11/99

D1169049

STAY!
Keeper's Story

OTHER YEARLING BOOKS YOU WILL ENJOY:

ANASTASIA AGAIN!, *Lois Lowry*
ANASTASIA, ABSOLUTELY!, *Lois Lowry*
ALL ABOUT SAM, *Lois Lowry*
ATTABOY, SAM!, *Lois Lowry*
NUMBER THE STARS, *Lois Lowry*
LILY'S CROSSING, *Patricia Reilly Giff*
DOUBLE ACT, *Jacqueline Wilson*
OLA SHAKES IT UP, *Joanne Hyppolite*
DON'T SPLIT THE POLE: TALES OF DOWN-HOME FOLK WISDOM,
Eleanora E. Tate
BOX TOP DREAMS, *Miriam Glassman*
THE ROBBER AND ME, *Josef Holub*

YEARLING BOOKS are designed especially to entertain and enlighten young people. Patricia Reilly Giff, consultant to this series, received her bachelor's degree from Marymount College and a master's degree in history from St. John's University. She holds a Professional Diploma in Reading and a Doctorate of Humane Letters from Hofstra University. She was a teacher and reading consultant for many years, and is the author of numerous books for young readers.

STAY!

Keeper's Story

LOIS LOWRY

Illustrated by True Kelley

THOMAS LAKE ELEM. IMC
4350 THOMAS LAKE ROAD
EAGAN, MN 55122-1840

A YEARLING BOOK

Published by
Bantam Doubleday Dell Books for Young Readers
a division of
Random House, Inc.
1540 Broadway
New York, New York 10036

If you purchased this book without a cover you should be aware that this book is
stolen property. It was reported as "unsold and destroyed" to the publisher and
neither the author nor the publisher has received any payment for this "stripped
book."

Text copyright © 1997 by Lois Lowry
Illustrations © 1997 by True Kelley

All rights reserved. No part of this book may be reproduced or transmitted in any
form or by any means, electronic or mechanical, including photocopying, record-
ing, or by any information storage and retrieval system, without the written per-
mission of the Publisher, except where permitted by law. For information
address Houghton Mifflin Company, 215 Park Avenue South, New York, New
York 10003.

The trademarks Yearling® and Dell® are registered in the U.S. Patent and
Trademark Office and in other countries.

Visit us on the Web! www.randomhouse.com

**Educators and librarians, for a variety of teaching tools,
visit us at www.randomhouse.com/teachers**

ISBN: 0-440-41524-1

Reprinted by arrangement with Houghton Mifflin Company

Printed in the United States of America

April 1999

10 9 8 7 6 5 4 3 2

CWO

For Susan Young
with thanks

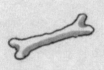

1

I WAS BORN IN THE GUTTER and grew up in poverty, abandoned by my parents, stealing and begging in order to survive. Then, through chance and circumstance, combined with (forgive my immodesty) a keen wit and a glorious appearance, I rose to grand heights of fame and affluence. Finally I retired to a quiet life in the country, surrounded by loved ones.

My story sounds familiar. Perhaps I remind the reader of someone who might once have run successfully for high public office.

But no; politics was not an avenue open to me, despite my gift for language and my affection for humanity. I am not human myself. I am of the family Canidae, a species depicted on the walls of the earliest caves and an accompaniment to history throughout the ages. You know me by my more common name, dog.

However, let me be clear about this. I do not like being referred to as The Dog.

I have a name.

The truth is, I have had several names. I hang my head a bit, recounting this history, because my beginnings could be called . . . well, sordid. But this is true of many dogs. Unlike the human population, dogs tend to be born in less than antiseptic places: under garages, surrounded by rusted tricycles and discarded two-by-fours slick with blue-green lichen; or behind a forgotten, moldy heap of outgrown clothing in a spiderwebbed corner of a damp cellar.

I was born, the second of four, between a board fence at the end of an alley and a set of trash cans beside the back door of a French restaurant named Toujours Cuisine. My mother had selected the location because of its proximity to food at a time when she, heavy with puppy, no longer felt like roaming the streets and back yards in search of morsels and handouts. She was exhausted and needed a resting place. The corner between the fence and the trash cans was quiet, dark, private, and unclaimed. A cat had lived there for a while; my mother, sniffing, could identify the former occupant as Cat, Male, No Longer Nearby.

So she squatted carefully and marked the place several times around its perimeter. Then she circled, pawing at the small bits of trash, smoothing the crumpled papers, and arranging the space. I was not there to observe, of course, prior to my own arrival, but I look back now and can visualize the ritual, since it is always the same in the world of the dog:

the careful arrangement, the meticulous preparation of the birthing place.

A week, or perhaps ten days, later, I was born, one of three brothers and followed by a small and fragile sister.

Only one of my littermates is by my side today, and after a long and difficult separation. Where are the others? I wish I knew. But it is the way of the dog that we separate from our kin and make our own way in the world. I remember only that we played and fought as infants, practicing our growls, learning our various postures and ear placements, each with its own coded meaning, and chewing each other's still undeveloped tails. I recall our nudging each other aside in our quest for the perfect nipple, the one with the best footing, the most abundant and dependable flow of lunch. We yipped and quarreled and our mother watched us with weary fondness, reaching out with one large paw from time to time to drag us back when we wandered on our wobbly legs too far from the curve of her belly.

We slept in a pile, warm against each other and all of us encircled by our mother, comforted by the deep rhythm of her heartbeat and rocked by the gentle heave of her body as she breathed.

Now and then she stood, stretched, and shook us loose. One brother in particular had such a strong, determined mouth that he dangled, feet waving, in the air, still attached, until Mom reached around impatiently, pried him away, and let him drop.

Then she would leave us alone. It is one of my first memories: the little chorus of whimpers, the squirming frenzy of our group as we sought to be cozy without her and cried with fear that she might not return.

As the days passed and I was able to open my eyes and focus clearly, I watched my mother's route when she abandoned us there briefly and set out on her own.

She went first to the door of the restaurant. It was not the front door (which later, when I was old enough to explore on my own, I found to be elaborately carved wood adorned with a brass plaque, very pretentious), but an unobtrusive back door, often left open so that kitchen employees could emerge and stand beside it, puffing on cigarettes and complaining about the head chef.

Sometimes the head chef himself emerged alone for a breath of air, a respite from the clatter of pans and the noisy quarrels of dishwashers and salad chefs. He would slump against the wall in despair, take a deep breath, and mutter in French.

"Mon dieu," I would hear him say. Or *"Sacrebleu,"* thinking himself quite alone, unaware that an attentive and, if I do say so myself, intelligent puppy was listening and absorbing the nuances of human speech. Then the chef would stand up straight, pull himself together, sigh, and return to the kitchen to right whatever cooking disaster had occurred.

If the door was closed, Mother would arrange herself in a sitting position beside it. Sometimes she tapped on it in a scratching gesture with her right front paw. But more often she had only to sit, in a pretty and appealing way, looking both worthy and in need. (It is a look that all dogs perfect, over the years, but I have to say that I have never seen it performed better than by my mother.)

She was, in fact, a handsome bitch. There was probably some collie in her past. She had the aristocratic nose of a fine collie — not mentioning any names, but you all know who comes to mind — but unlike collies, Mother had an attractive curl to her amber fur. I was born with the same natural

10

and copious curl. My two brothers, less favored in looks, had straight hair, and my sister — we called her Wispy — had a coat that was unfortunately sparse, with a mottled patch on one shoulder. Her personality was lively and appealing, but for much of her life, until fate changed her luck, potential suitors, human and dog, never seemed to see beyond what I once heard referred to as a "mangy" (forgive me; it is not a word I like to repeat) look.

But Mother was, as I have said, a magnificent bitch. Her manners were impeccable. And she had perfected the posture (chin up, tail at rest, head cocked) and expression (solemn, luminous eyes) that combined disdain and necessity. Invariably someone smiled, said "Just a minute, I'll get

you something," and brought an unscraped plate: morsels of *poulet roti*, crisp with buttery skin (quite good for the glisten of one's fur), an occasional tournedo still sporting coagulated béarnaise. I watched from my place, nestled against my littermates, amazed to see how daintily Mother licked the sauce

11

away before nibbling the chicken or beef with fastidious little bites. I knew how famished she was. I could hear, from my spot against her belly, how her insides grumbled with hunger. But she was a dignified dog; and she was a clever one, as well. She knew that manners defined her future, and that tearing at the leftovers with ravenous greed would have prevented her from receiving the respect that a fine crossbreed mostly collie deserves. So she concealed her hunger with an utmost effort of will and toyed with the leftovers from a fifty-dollar French meal. Then finally, with a resigned sigh that said, "An adequate dinner, though I've had better in my day," she would swallow the last herbed morsel, toss her tail prettily from one side to the other, and stroll away.

My mother knew how to play to an audience.

From the fine dinner at the restaurant kitchen's door she would wander on, alert, to the main street, where one could scavenge occasional dropped treasures: a melting ice cream cone on the pavement, not a bad dessert for a dog, or greasy paper once wrapped around a hamburger, not a bad thing to lick.

Then she would return to our hidden dwelling, circle carefully so as not to flatten us, and lie down. We would toddle over and lick her face, tasting the remains of her meal. Wispy and I savored the different tastes attached to Mother's chin and whiskers, but our brothers pushed us aside, growling, scolding Mother for not saving larger portions for her children.

The differences between us began to be clear. My two brothers had from birth been relentlessly energetic and quarrelsome. They nipped at each other endlessly, shoving and pushing, making life into an exhausting contest. Inevitably they extended playful wrestling matches into real battles, until Wispy and I scampered whimpering to our mother to be licked and calmed.

My mother gave them pet names that reflected their contentious personalities. Tug and Tussle, she called them.

One day, as the boys were quarreling in a corner near the trash cans while I lay quietly with Wispy, enjoying a patch of sunshine that had worked its way around the side of the building, I said casually to my sister, "Listen to Thug and Muscle."

Wispy, who had been half asleep, opened her eyes. She giggled. "Thug and Muscle?"

I had surprised myself. "It just came out that way," I told her.

"Cute," Wispy said, and closed her eyes again.

I said it to myself several times, liking the sound of it, the way Tug turned into Thug and Tussle into Muscle. It *was* cute. Stretching there in the sun, listening to the boys fight, I tried a few more experiments with human words.

"Yip," I whispered to myself, as one of my brothers punctuated the morning with a small half-bark.

"Nip," I added, identifying the reason for his little pained sound.

"Grr," I said to myself thoughtfully. Then, after pondering for a moment, I added, with satisfaction, "Fur."

"Wake up, Wispy!" I urged my sister. "Listen to what I can do!"

She opened her eyes, yawned patiently, and listened while I explained to her how I was putting words together into rhymes. "What rhymes with cheese?" she asked me, and her little tail thumped against the ground. Wispy loved cheese more than anything.

I thought long and hard. Finally I whispered a hideous

13

word to her, a word that Mother preferred us not to use. "Fleas," I said in a very low voice. Wispy shuddered.

"Sorry," I said quickly. "*Peas* would rhyme," I added after a moment. Wispy sighed. Neither of us was very fond of peas — or *pois,* as they were called in French. I don't think Mother was either. She usually nosed them around on the plate, as if she were looking for something better.

As we grew, we began to yearn for more than milk and occasional licks of buttery smears on Mother's face. The sporadic tidbits that she brought us were tantalizing hints that a greater world of food lay somewhere just beyond our reach.

One morning my first-born brother, the one we called Tug, decided to leave our hiding place and go out to forage on his own. We were alone at the time. Mother had gone on one of her own food-finding forays. Now that we were no longer babies, Mother was gone more and more, and for longer and longer periods.

I watched apprehensively as Tug ventured forth. He was not my favorite of my siblings. I much preferred to play with gentle Wispy, or even with Tussle, who was boisterous but good-natured and meant no harm. But Tug was my brother, after all, so I wished him well.

He trotted over to the restaurant door, sat in the place where Mother always sat, assumed the pose that Mother used, and woofed lightly. Mother never barked; eloquent silence was her way. But impatience was part of Tug's nature.

His bark was small, since he was young, but it did bring one of the dishwashers to the door. He was a heavyset man called Pete; I had seen him often, wiping his hands on the dirty white apron he wore, reaching into a pocket for a crumpled pack of cigarettes. He had an interesting decoration, a

14

dagger entwined with flowers, all in purple, extending from his wrist halfway up his arm. He had a loud laugh.

Pete laughed now, looking down at my brother.

"Hey, look here!" he called back through the open doorway into the kitchen. "She's got a puppy!"

The other dishwashers appeared, each wiping his damp hands. They all looked down at Tug, who was trying to maintain his jaunty appearance, though I could tell, because I

knew him well, that he was nervous. His tail was quivering slightly, and his ears — still puppy ears and therefore not completely under his command — were not entirely erect.

Pete squatted and picked him up. For a human with such large hands and such a loud voice, he was surprisingly gentle, and he knew to cradle Tug's bottom in the palm of his hand. I could tell, though, how frightened my brother must be, suddenly for the first time ascending into the air with his thin legs dangling. I could see his brown eyes peering down in panic.

Then I heard a roar of human laughter.

"Gotcha, Pete!" one of the dishwashers called.

"Look at that," Pete said. "Peed right into my hand!"

It confirmed what I had guessed: that Tug was frightened. No self-confident dog would have lost control that way.

"Lemme see it," one of them, a thin black man, said. He took Tug from Pete, who rubbed his damp hand on his apron. "I've been promising my kid a puppy. Is this male or female?" I could see him lift my brother's little tail and peer at his bottom.

The four men all leaned over and peered. There is an amazing lack of privacy in a dog's life.

"Female," one said finally.

"Yeah, female," the others agreed.

Oh, the humiliation I felt on Tug's behalf.

"If you don't want her for your kid, I'll take her home. My girlfriend wants a dog," the tallest man said. "And she said she wants a female."

"Females are gentler. Females never bite," Pete announced, as if he were the voice of wisdom. I realized then what a fool he was. There was no truth at all to what he said.

"I want her," the thin black man decided.

16

I don't know if Tug understood this conversation and knew that his fate was being determined. It takes a while for a dog to learn the language of humans, and Tug was not the most intelligent of our litter. I am not inclined to vanity. But I will explain that my sister, Wispy, was not much interested in study or education. She had listened politely to my delighted discovery of rhyme and had asked a few cordial questions, but Wispy was hardly a scholar. And of my two brothers, Tug, the elder and braver, was . . . well, all right, I'll say it — not at all bright. Tussle, the playful one, had an endearing love of a good romp and a more congenial personality than Tug, but no intellectual curiosity at all.

No, it was I alone among my litter who had paid attention to the nuances of human speech. It was I who understood exactly what the dishwashers were saying as they passed Tug around and planned his future.

And I knew what the words meant when I heard Pete say, "If there's one puppy, there'll be more! Let's take a look!"

I had just a few seconds to hide under the corner of a nearby flattened cardboard carton, but there was no time to waken and warn my remaining brother or my sister as the quartet of aproned men approached our secret home in search of pets.

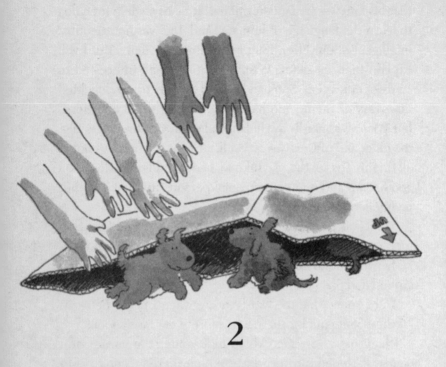

2

I LAY TREMBLING UNDER THE DAMP, warped cardboard, trying to make myself small. I *was* small, of course, still a partially grown pup. Though we were clearly descended from distinguished members of herding and hunting breeds (none of those miniatures or toys designed only for laps were in our background, I am certain), I was still of a size that could be held in one large human hand. And I was frighteningly aware that several sets of such hands were approaching my hiding place. I tried to make myself invisible by stretching my body and legs out as flat as possible. Suddenly I experienced once again an impulse toward poetry, born of panic.

Flee! Flee! Flee! were the words that came to my mind as I cringed there in terror. Then, unbidden, they were followed by *Gotta pee! Gotta pee!* and though it was true enough, my physical urge brought on by fear, what caught my attention was the sound of the rhyme. For a brief second I almost forgot my precarious position as I felt a desire to play more with the words, to rearrange them in a more pleasing way. But the danger that confronted me won out, and I postponed any poetic yearnings in order to concentrate on remaining hidden. I thought nervously about my tail.

I was not certain whether my tail was exposed. Surprisingly, a dog does not have much awareness of his own tail. Pride in it, certainly; my own, though still young and incomplete, was beginning to show signs of developing into a particularly magnificent tail, fringed and straight. But awareness of its minute-to-minute placement was difficult to achieve without actually turning around to look and assess.

"Here they are!" It was the voice of Pete.

"Looky there. I *thought* she was eating a lot." The thin black man was speaking. His voice was not at all cruel, just concerned.

I did not dare to peek. They were quite near. I hoped my tail, if it was exposed, would not move and betray me. Considering its importance as an appendage, the sad lack of control over one's tail is astounding.

I could hear the men talking. "Counting the one Pete's got, three of them little buggers. They're cute, aren't they?"

"Maybe I'll take two home instead of just the one. Whaddaya think? Will my girlfriend kill me if I take two?"

"Nah. Women like puppies. She'll start talking babytalk to them the minute you walk through the door."

"Find me another female, would you?"

I waited, shivering and listening, as they picked up Tussle and Wispy. I pictured the embarrassing scrutiny taking place.

Then I cringed, crouching there under the cardboard; and probably my tail, unwilled by my brain, wiggled in humiliation for my brothers (and I was glad that they had not learned the nuances of human speech, and so would not know) as once again the dishwashers, almost in unison, pronounced each puppy to be female.

I heard the men gather them up. I heard the frightened whimpers. I did nothing. What could I do? I stayed hidden.

I have carried that guilt with me all my life.

"This one don't look too good," someone said. I knew he must be referring to Wispy. Her fur was so discolored and sparse. I would like to think there was compassion in his voice.

"Ah, bring it along. If nobody wants it, we'll drop it off at the animal shelter."

My heart leaped. I knew the word *shelter* and that it meant, for humans at least, food and clothing and a bed. Sometimes, on rainy nights, several human occupants of the alley where I had lived since my birth decided to go to "the shelter." It was crowded, I had heard them say, noisier than they liked, and lacking in privacy, but in times of stress and need, it was a place of comfort and respite.

I had not known that there was an animal shelter, too.

"Yeah," I heard Pete say as they headed toward the restaurant door, their aprons weighted with puppies. "They'll put it to sleep at the shelter."

I was relieved. Maybe, I thought, I should have revealed myself and gone along. To be put to sleep — after some food and perhaps warm milk and some playtime — sounded like an appealing thing, and would no doubt involve some nice ragged blankets, free of fleas.

I wriggled free of my cardboard and scampered toward the restaurant door.

"Wait!" I yipped. "I was here all along! I'm part of the group! Can I go? Can I be put to sleep?"

But the door had closed.

Night was coming, I noticed.

Sadly I plodded back to the corner behind the trash cans. I curled up, my tail all the way around to my chin, and tried to get comfy. I began to play with rhyming words again.

> *All alone! What to do?*
> *Brothers gone! Sister, also!*

Very quickly, thinking it over, I realized my mistake and corrected it to *Sister, too!* How pleasant it sounded, with the words in order, and in rhyme. What a comfort poetry could be in one's life. At that point, cold and lonely, I needed what comfort I could find.

Mother had been away for hours. She had never left us for such a long time before. As much as I longed for her, and her warm belly to sleep against, and the supply of milk that it always provided, I dreaded seeing her face when she returned and found her babies gone.

Finally, still waiting, I dozed off.

* * *

I woke again, chilly, sometime in the night. I wiggled my nose and sniffed Essence of Mother, that particularly reassuring smell that said she was nearby. But the familiar scent seemed slightly different. It was mingled with Essence of Other Dog, Male. Puzzled, I yawned, sneezed once, and raised my head to look around.

There she was, at the end of the alley. I stretched, tiptoed over to the side of the trash can, and peered around to get a good look. My mother was standing there with a tall, dark, and handsome Doberman. She was . . . well, I guess the only word would be *flirting*. Her tail was moving with a very contrived swish, and she arched her neck to rub against the Doberman's sleek shoulders. It was cheap, trashy behavior, in my opinion, and I was shocked to see it.

I whimpered and she glanced my way. I am quite certain she saw me. Her left ear twitched.

I tried a small bark. Now her escort, the Doberman, looked over at me with bored eyes. Impatiently he turned back to her, and she sighed. They nuzzled each other for a moment more; then he turned and trotted away while Mother watched.

Quickly I scampered back to the hidden place, flopped down, and pretended to be asleep. I waited. I could hear her approaching, but her steps were slow and reluctant. In the past she had always hurried back to us, checked out our well-being with an affectionate nose, and arranged herself protectively around our little group.

Now, though, she sighed and pawed restlessly at the ground, barely seeming to notice me. I had thought I would comfort her in her grief at the loss of the other puppies. But she seemed not to be aware that they were gone. She looked longingly at the corner behind which the Doberman had disappeared.

I whimpered again slightly, but she paid no attention, and I did not want to seem like a whiner. Finally she settled restlessly beside me, acknowledging that her evening on the town was over.

I sensed that she was bored with motherhood and eager to resume life as a party girl. I didn't blame her, really; she was young yet — only three, I think — and in the way of dogs still had ahead of her a lifetime of flirtations, love affairs, and no doubt (though I did not want to think about it) other puppies yet to come.

I licked one paw, pretending to be very concerned about a small bit of damp newsprint stuck to my fur, and glanced at her to see if she was interested in my grooming, as she once would have been. She tended to me in a businesslike way, but her thoughts were clearly elsewhere.

Did she not notice that her puppies were gone? I think she did, in truth. She pawed a bit at the sleeping place, puzzled by the change. Then she seemed to accept things as they were. She sighed, sat tensely for a moment, then relaxed into a sleeping position, and finally closed her eyes and slept. I did the same, but my dreams were anxious and uncertain: dreams about finding my own way in the world; dreams about being all alone.

When morning came, I knew that my dream had been more than that. It had been an omen. My mother's sleeping place was empty. In the intuitive way of dogs, I realized that she would not be back.

Seeking solace, I tried to write an ode to Mother but found I could not finish. Everything I composed ended with the word *alone,* and the only rhyme I could think of was *bone.*

The more I thought of *bone,* the less I thought about Mother. I realized, as my attention turned to urgent needs, that I was very hungry. My nose twitched. Suddenly I sniffed, from some unexplored place around the corner, something that might well be breakfast.

Unbidden, new poetry came to me:

> *Upright, my tail! Forward, my legs!*
> *I think I smell some ham and biscuits!*

No, of course, it had to be *eggs!* I began to see how poetry worked. I said the couplet again to myself with satisfaction and new energy. It sounded like an anthem or a marching song. It cheered me. Orphaned now, but not overwhelmed, I turned my back on my past and set forth.

3

AT THE CORNER OF THE ALLEY I stopped. Ahead of me lay a busy street, not at all like the quiet, neglected place that had been my home for all of my previous life. In the way of dogs, I sniffed cautiously. I erected my ears to their maximum alertness and tilted my head to listen.

Mother had taught us each scrupulously about the use of senses. "Nose, ears, eyes," she had said again and again, so that we would memorize the correct order of importance. Nose, ears, eyes. It sounds easy. But my less bright brothers had tended to look and leap without stopping to sniff and listen. Mother had reminded them with increasing impatience.

I could almost hear her voice reminding me now.

Nose. I could smell gasoline exhaust: great gagging bursts from the back of a large bus that moved away from the curb to my right. I caught a whiff of newsprint quite nearby, and turned my head to see a folded paper in the entrance of a building to my left. As I assessed the paper, congratulating my nose a bit, I sniffed Male Human, and indeed was able to congratulate my accuracy again as a man opened a door, stepped outside, and leaned down to pick up the folded newspaper.

The scent of his stale tobacco-tinged breath was familiar to me from the dishwashers who often smoked beside the restaurant's back door. I brought my ears into play, aimed them toward the man, and heard the scratch and flare of a match as he lit up and drew deeply on the cigarette. Then he took himself, his scent, and the aroma of newspaper and cigarette back into the building and behind its closed door. A slight odor remained, but the freshness, the sharp pungency, was gone.

Breakfast. The scents that had attracted me were still there, drifting in from a distance, and I was still very hungry. *"Forward, legs . . ."* my poetic voice was still saying.

But I knew I should be wary. A dog's life is fraught with potential danger: from Car, from Cat, from Man, from Hostile Dog, and from all the frightening subcategories therein.

So I proceeded with utmost caution. Sniffing, listening, and watching in all directions, I ventured forth around the corner and along the sidewalk that bordered the busy street.

Inching my way carefully past a wheeled vehicle containing a baby, I was startled when a sticky hand reached out and grabbed my left ear. It was my first experience of being

touched by a human, and I did not like it very much. Of
course it was a subhuman, being only an infant; nonetheless,
its grab hurt. An ear is a very delicate thing.

I confess that I yipped.

"Max!" its mother shrieked, and removed its hand from me
in an alarmed fashion. I was not surprised. It was an alarming
event, the possible damage to my ear. In addition, the baby's
hand was not at all clean. It was filled with half-chewed
cookie.

"Never, never touch a dog!" the mother said in a firm,
frightened voice.

I liked that mother. She understood the grave potential
danger to my ear.

The baby waved its hands about, paying no attention what-soever to its mother. It behaved in much the same manner as my brothers, frisking about and not listening to instructions. My heart went out to that wonderful mother, trying so nobly to explain to her child the rules of kindness to dogs.

"Max?" the mother said sternly. "Are you listening to me?"

Pay attention, Max, I commanded under my breath. *She is teaching you valuable lessons about the importance of being both gentle and generous to dogs. Listen.*

The baby stared at his mother. He had rather bulbous eyes, and there was dried mucus, nostril in origin, encrusted on his upper lip. He was not well groomed. His fingernails were dirty, and he was arranging his right index finger into a pointing position, clearly planning to poke me some place exquisitely painful on my face.

"Dogs are filthy creatures, Max!" the mother said, to my astonishment. "They're nasty! They carry diseases! And they bite!" she added untruthfully.

I hardly knew how to react to such glaring deceit. Finally I decided that the only dignified response would be to walk away.

First, though, since he was still waving his hand about, I bent over, took Max's half-eaten cookie in my mouth, and consumed it in one gulp. Then I flipped my young but already glorious tail to one side with disdain and continued on without looking back.

The smell of breakfast was coming from a fast-food place down the street. Eagerly I made my way along the sidewalk, around humans carrying packages. There were no other babies, for which I was grateful, having learned how ruthless they are, and the humans I passed ignored me. They seemed busy, hurried, and distracted.

Each human I passed emitted a variety of scents. The basic scent that said Human was primary and strongest, of course, and overlaid with the secondary scent of Male or Female. But these were covered superficially by a medley of soaps, perfumes, powders, cosmetics, shampoos, and the remains of many different breakfasts. Some were new and foreign to me. But I recognized others, taught to me by my mom: butter, for example, which had so often coated her lips after she had dined by the French restaurant's back door.

Cream, too, was familiar, as was coffee, which I did not like. I recognized bacon and bread, and soap was not new to me either. The hands of the dishwashers, the very hands that had carried away my puppy brothers and sister, were permeated with the fragrant, antiseptic odor of soap.

Perfume was unpleasant, and I wondered why females used it. In the dog world, there is no more pleasing scent to a male than the natural and undiminished bouquet of a female. Some, of course, are more appealing than others. Female poodles are not particularly appetizing, except perhaps to male poodles; I do not know why.

Most small breeds — Yorkie, Maltese, and the Dandie Dinmont — tend to have a perky and amusing aroma. Golden retrievers have a wonderfully warm and earthy scent, and a Newfoundland smells of the sea. At the time of which I am telling, I had not yet encountered many breeds of dog; those days, those meetings, were yet to come. But I did notice, setting forth on my first day as an independent, newly motherless being, the quite overwhelming fragrances with which humans tried to disguise their natural scents. No self-respecting dog would use perfume, I thought with a somewhat superior toss of my head as I trotted through the pungent crowd.

Upright, my tail! Forward, my feet!
Prepare, teeth! We approach hamburger!

Of course I realized instantly that the second line should conclude with the word *meat*. Feeling that I was maturing as a poet, I repeated the verse in its revised, rhyming version as I approached the shop from which the smells were drifting. I ignored the humans lined up in front of the counter, where people wearing odd paper hats were taking their orders, and made my way craftily toward the back door. My mother had taught me well, especially about the location and acquisition of food. The back rooms of restaurants, populated by somewhat bored and often good-natured employees, had back doors, which were frequently open.

It was at such an open door that a needy dog should sit. I made my way there, reciting my poem to myself, rehearsing in my mind the sort of polite, wistful posture and expression I would use: the slight cock to the head, the wide eyes. I would not unless absolutely necessary raise my paws to a begging position. Mother had found such a pose demeaning — though on occasion she had been forced to use it — and I wanted to honor her memory.

Following the aroma of cooking and the cries of "Egg McMuffin!" and "Black coffee coming up!" I approached the back door. Indeed, as I had hoped, it was open.

Unfortunately, a terrifying rival had gotten there first. The flat-faced dog I confronted was well muscled and broad of chest; his short white fur was mottled with dirt. His eyes were red-rimmed, and a thick scar, jagged but well healed, on the side of his face pulled his lip askew, giving him the appearance of a perpetual snarl.

Upright my fur! Be brave, O pup! I said nervously to my-self, feeling the hairs on my back bristle in apprehension, and failing to finish the poem. Mother had told me about Hostile Dogs; she had listed them among Things to Be Feared.

She was right. I feared him a *lot*. He was large, determined, and defiant. By contrast, I was small, uncertain, and fearful.

But we were both hungry.

His scent — possessive and alert — said that it was *his* restaurant door. His eyes glittered, watching me as I tiptoed very slowly forward. His tail (a stump, quite unattractive), resting behind him on the ground, moved slowly from one side to the other: not a friendly wag at all, but a symbol of antagonism and threat.

I bowed a bit, acknowledging his superior size and the fact that he was first in line. But I did not retreat. I was too hungry to retreat.

His upper lip moved slightly, exposing his teeth. They were rather good teeth for a dog: even and sharp, nicely yellowed and worn, with long fangs on either side.

I still had my pointed baby teeth, quite new little biters that had served me well, and thought he might like to know that. So I raised my lip at him.

Scar (for I had named him, in my mind) stood before me in a pose of unrelenting threat, and his growl was steady.

We faced each other, and I feel that I was brave in my stance. But it was no contest. He was much larger and more experienced than I. Finally I retreated, moving backward slowly.

Staring at him in my retreat, I memorized his face and knew that someday I would see it again. He was not the sort of enemy who would disappear. I resolved that our next meeting would have a different outcome.

But for now I was the loser. When I had backed far enough to be out of his immediate realm, I turned around, still in a humiliated, beaten posture. But as I left the back of the restaurant and the passageway that led to it and its wealth of discarded food, I gathered my courage long enough to give one last flippant gesture. I raised my right leg and made my mark against the wall that defined his space.

Then I tossed my head and trotted hungrily away, knowing at least that Scar would have to live with my scent for a long time. Somehow that knowledge made my defeat more bearable.

4

I NEEDED A CHILD.

My mother had taught me that all puppies need children.

Adults are strict with their dogs, insisting that they eat designated food — usually not very tasty — from a particular bowl, often heavy and unattractive. Adults make their dogs sleep in not very cozy places: basements, garages, or wire cages (and they tell their human friends: "He loves his cage," which is not true, not one bit true), or sometimes on a flea-retardant dog bed stuffed with cedar shavings.

Dogs would much rather eat dog-sized portions of human meals; pasta is a particular favorite. They would like it served on a dinner plate placed on the floor near the human table.

Instead of a cage as a refuge, dogs like a nice little cedar house with a pointed roof and a small entrance with the dog's name painted in big letters over it.

Dogs prefer to sleep snuggled right up beside a human, their head on a feather pillow, with ears nicely spread out, and the rest of the body curled on an innerspring mattress covered by percale sheets smelling of human breath and sweat.

Children understand all of that. I wanted a child. But there were none in sight.

Back on the main street, I watched the brisk crowd of humans going about their day. It made no sense to attach myself to the side of a human with a briefcase, though there were many such, both male and female. They entered the doors of large buildings and pushed buttons summoning noisy mechanical cages, into which they disappeared.

Suddenly I spotted one man who did appeal to me. He was dressed in a multi-aromaed collection of clothing, and his beard — for he had a long, uncombed one — smelled of several past meals. He was not hurrying. He seemed, in fact, to have no destination at all. He simply stood beside the wall of a building, talking to himself. His hand was cupped in front of him, and occasionally someone dropped a coin into it. "Money for coffee? Money for coffee?" he was saying to the passersby. "Bless you, bless you," he murmured when a coin was dropped into his hand.

I liked his smells. No soap, no shampoo, no toothpaste, no aftershave. Just coffee and tobacco and dirt: a wonderfully earthy combination, layered over by a whiff of old doughnut and some stale hamburger.

I went and arranged myself unobtrusively by his side.

When he reached down and scratched me behind one ear, I knew that he was the next best thing to a child.

"Good boy, good boy," he said to me. He seemed to say everything twice, but I didn't mind. At least he had not called me "Good girl," a lapse I didn't think I would tolerate as cordially as my brothers had.

Tentatively I licked his hand. Aside from the repellent infant, Max, whose hand had been gluey with mashed cookie, this was my first taste of human flesh. The man's hand tasted of many things, some of them edible.

> *O hand of man! My first to lick!*
> *O dirt! O beer! O licorice stick!*

In truth, I was not positive that it was licorice stick I tasted. I think it might have been cough syrup. But I was learning, even at this earliest stage in my literary career, that a poet may take some license, may stray lightly from absolute truth, if the verse seems to demand it.

The man reached into the pocket of the outermost coat that he was wearing (there seemed to be at least two others underneath) and held a morsel of something mysterious under my mouth. I was too hungry to investigate it carefully. I gulped it down and looked longingly at him, wondering if his other pockets held more.

"Sorry boy, sorry boy," he told me. I sighed.

"Feed a hungry puppy? Feed a hungry puppy?" he began to say in his singsong voice. To my surprise, people stopped, looked at me, smiled, and dropped money into his hand. Now and then someone patted my head.

Pasta? I thought. Stew? I remembered all the things Mother had described: the human foods that best suited a dog. Vegetable soup? I wondered where we would go shopping for my meal. My new friend was dropping coins into his pocket, then holding his empty hand out again and repeating his phrase, entreating the passing humans to donate to my welfare.

He shook his jingling pocket and patted my head happily. "Sit," he murmured to me. "Sit."

I decided to do exactly as he said. We were still quite close to the fast-food place from which I had fled so ignominiously, and I felt that I needed a protector in case Scar should come looking for me, since I had, after all, defaced his territory.

In addition, it was clear that the man planned to feed me. I decided to walk politely by his heel when we went to the grocery store. Judging by the number of coins in his pocket now, it wouldn't be long. We had enough money for a substantial amount of grocery shopping.

"What's his name?" a woman asked, searching in her purse for some change.

My new friend looked down at me. I sat with my best posture, tilted my head, and waited to hear his answer. A name is an important thing, and except for little endearments from my mother and sister, I had not had one until now.

"Lucky," he told the woman. "Lucky."

Creativity overwhelmed me, and I began to compose.

> *Lucky I am, and Lucky I'll be!*
> *O lucky lucky lucky me!*

It was not one of my finest poems. But it was the first to incorporate my name, and I had composed it quickly in my surge of tender appreciation that I had a human of my own. I wondered if he had soft sheets on his bed, and perhaps a thick quilt that smelled of spilled leftovers. I felt immensely happy and poetic, and resolved that my next ode would be better than *Lucky I am*, which I knew to be inadequate.

I was to be disappointed, at the end of the day, in most of my expectations. In the evening he led me to his home, and it was barely superior to the one I had left. My last resting place had been under a piece of corrugated cardboard in a dirty alley. This man's home was on a riverbank, below a bridge, under a large piece of flattened tin.

"Here we are, Lucky," he said as he lifted a corner of the tin and indicated that I should enter, with a somewhat courtly gesture of his hand. Then he made a small fire and heated some of the cans of food that he had bought with the coins from his day's collection.

Together we dined.

"My name's Jack," he told me, and I was touched by the introduction, since most humans do not bother with such courtesies toward dogs. Even in my short and unsophisticated life to date, I had observed that there is a brusqueness toward dogs. "Hey, boy!" is often used as a greeting, for example; and food, even the finest French food, is simply tossed on the ground toward its recipient. My mother, a fastidious female, commented on that. "You'd think," she said to me once while cleaning her paws and chin after a visit to Toujours Cuisine, "that they'd serve something as elegant as *saucisson en brioche* on a *plate*, at least."

I didn't, of course, compare my first dinner with Jack to fine cuisine. It was shared stew from a can, with river water to wash it down for me and a beer for Jack, who burped afterward without apology. But there was a sweetness to the camaraderie, and I felt a sense of safety which made up for the lack of elegance. I curled beside him under the tin, and we slept soundly together, covered by an old army overcoat, frayed at the seams, which he tucked around us both.

O lucky lucky lucky me, I murmured to myself before I fell asleep.

5

I settled in and stayed with Jack, the man who called me Lucky. He was not always as honest as one would like a human to be, and he was not particularly clean, a thing that matters to dogs.

But he was kind. From his collected coins, he always purchased a can of dogfood first. (I preferred, actually, the beef stew intended for humans, but Jack thought that he was doing me a favor by purchasing food designated for dogs. It is a mistake that humans often make.) Then he stocked up on his own favorite treats, California jug wine and a bag of bacon curls. We dined together each evening, under the bridge. He always dipped a plastic bowl of water for me, from the river. I could easily have stood at the edge and lapped, but he seemed to like the niceties and the togetherness, so I drank from a bowl as he refreshed himself from the jug.

Sometimes he toasted me. "Here's to you, Lucky!" he would say affectionately, raising his jug toward the sky. Then he would scratch my ears, and I would lick his hand in acknowledgment.

At night I slept curled by his side, the two of us under the sheet of tin that he called home.

"I had a bed once, Lucky," he told me one evening as we arranged ourselves for sleep. "And a house. But things turned bad."

Having never lived in a house myself at that time, I probably did not fully appreciate the downward turn his life had taken. The tin roof over us, the plastic bowl, and the dependable can of food, though not a name brand and certainly nothing like the entrées from Toujours Cuisine, seemed home enough for me.

"Yessir," he said mournfully, "I had a home once. And a family."

I lamented with him the loss of family, having suffered through it myself. So I looked up at him mournfully, encouraging him to talk more.

"Yessir," Jack went on. "Had a wife once, Lucky. But just look what happens. You make a dumb mistake or two. Then it all falls apart."

He pulled the ragged overcoat around his shoulders and shifted on the hard ground, trying to get comfortable. I snuggled closer, to warm him. We dogs do not suffer much from the elements, furred and sturdy as we are. But the weather was turning colder now, and Jack seemed frail and easily chilled.

I wondered what his dumb mistake might have been. It could not have been worse than my own. I was haunted by the fact that, like a coward, I had concealed myself on that fateful day when my own family had disappeared. Every day I remembered and mourned my small sister, Wispy. I could still see the look in her brown eyes as she peered down uncomprehending from the arms of the man who had said he would arrange for her to be put to sleep.

I hoped her sleep, wherever it was, was comfortable and that she had someone who cared for her with the same tender concern I felt from the man who called me Lucky.

My own sleep was often interrupted. The place that Jack had chosen for a home, though scenic, with the river nearby, and convenient to the busy streets where he made his uncertain living, was not at all safe.

Among the persistent and irritating dangers were the rats. I knew about rats from the alley that had been my first home. They had been a constant source of concern for Mother when we were small, for the rats that had frequented the alley were actually larger than new puppies and might even have viewed us as food. Mother always growled and lunged ferociously into the dark corners before she settled us for sleep. Sometimes we would see one flee, its thin naked tail scuttling away in response to Mother's threat.

Once when Mother was away, I had actually rescued Wispy from a confrontation with a rat. The creature had advanced with stealth and taken my sister by surprise, cornering her. By the time I noticed the event unfolding, Wispy was paralyzed with fear and it appeared that the rat was about to pounce upon her and bite. I was still young, but I simply mimicked my mother, growling as ferociously as I could and lunging toward the yellow-eyed rodent. Fortunately, he was

41

taken by surprise and fled, for I do not know if I could, at that young age, have beaten him in a fight.

Now, of course, I was much larger. But the waterfront rats were larger, too. Jack laughed at them and shook the tin roof to make a rattling, thunderous noise, which startled them away. But they always waited, there in the distance immediately past the light of our evening fire, which reflected their eyes in the darkness. The empty unwashed cans from our dinners attracted them with the smell of food. Sometimes, while Jack slept, I would hear the clink of the metal containers as rodent life licked and bit at what few rotting morsels were left.

I stayed vigilant, even while sleeping, and the slightest noise startled me awake. Again and again, without his knowledge, I protected Jack as the rats approached in the dark. A menacing growl, I found, kept them at bay. But they were always there, waiting, and nighttime became an ongoing battleground.

Though my growth to adulthood enabled me to protect Jack from the rats, it meant that I was no longer as reliable a source of income for him. My puppy fluff coarsened into thick adult fur which was not as soft to touch, though it was handsome fur in its own right, I felt, much like my mother's. My legs, once stubby, grew long, and rather than stumbling cutely over my large feet, I had grown to fit them and taken on the stance and gait of a mature dog. My repertoire of cute puppy mannerisms, like the small frightened yip and the tiny playful growl, no longer attracted passersby to smile at me and drop quarters into the hat.

But Jack was clever. One morning he carefully straightened the bent earpiece of a pair of sunglasses he found in a trash can. He added a cane to his costume, and when we took our place on the street, he changed his chant. No longer "Food for a hungry puppy," now his appeal was "Feed my guide dog, feed my guide dog," and the coins flew again into the receptacle.

In a way it was not completely dishonest. More and more, as time passed, I did become his guide, even though he could see. He was not well at all. He coughed uncontrollably in the night and seemed to lose his appetite for food. His bacon curls went unconsumed, at least by him; for me, they became an extra helping of dinner, and I believe the grease gave an added sheen to my adult coat.

One cold night as Jack slept, shivering, and I lay beside him, watchful and worried, I heard a new sound out beyond the dark perimeter of our space. My ears came to an upright position and I listened alertly. There was the constant scuttle, hiss, and chatter of the rats. But a new sound had been added. I heard furtive, heavy movements in the dark.

I sniffed cautiously. The abundance of smells — garbage, rats, the heavy pungence of a discarded oil drum, and the on-going reek of the scummy river water — made it difficult to isolate and identify a new scent. But I lay very still, concentrating, using the full capacity of my ears and nose.

I knew suddenly that it was Scar. Since our initial encounter on the day I left home, almost a year had passed. But I had been imprinted then by an awareness of his power and potential for evil, and had encountered nothing since that had surpassed it.

What was he doing here?

Stealthily I wriggled out from under Jack's clasp, for he was sleeping heavily with his arm over my back and one hand draped across my neck. He didn't wake, though he stirred and coughed.

Then, with my body lowered close to the ground, I inched forward in the dark, away from the cover of the tin sheet that formed our roof. The smell of my enemy became intense in the frosty night air, overpowering the stench of the rats, who seemed to have backed away, retreating to their home in the sewer pipe at the edge of the river. Very slowly I crept forward. I could see him now, his thick ungainly body outlined against the dark sky. I could hear the snap of his jaws as he tore at some edible object. In the frenzy of his eating, he was unaware of me.

So he had not come looking for me; he was not here to settle an old score, but simply because he had found some sort of meal that happened to be on my turf. I had a chance to take him by surprise.

I gathered myself, both courage and muscles, then sprang at Scar, landing on his broad back. Surprised, he dropped his meal and wrestled us both to the ground, his heavy jaws snapping as he tried again and again to grab my throat. He was still larger than I. But I was agile and quick and managed to keep clear of his grip. We fought silently in the night, the only sounds our panting breath and the occasional low growls from both of our throats. I felt blood flow when he bit my back, but I think that I injured him as well, with a quick snap to his ear that left me with bloodied fur in my mouth.

No one won. We both paused at last, exhausted, and he took advantage of the intermission in the battle. While I rested briefly, Scar grabbed the carcass on which he'd been feeding; I could see now that it was the body of a large rat. With the remains dangling from his mouth, Scar turned and loped away without looking back.

I limped back to our lean-to and huddled beside Jack in the dim light of early dawn. I assessed my wounds and licked my stained and spattered fur clean. The sky was pale gray, and it looked as if it might rain. The river surged relentlessly on, carrying with it all manner of filth. I watched the rats emerge nervously from the sewer, eyes aglitter and tails darting. Scar had disappeared, but there was a splotch of gore where he had been feasting on rodent.

The world seemed utterly miserable to me on that grim dawn, and I am not ashamed to say that I whimpered like a puppy in my despair. Gradually Jack woke. He stroked my neck and said "Lucky" in an affectionate tone, and I was glad that he had not seen what I had of the cruelty and foulness that surrounded us in the night.

I nudged Jack awake each morning and urged him up, but as time passed he seemed less eager to be out and about. His *joie de vivre* seemed to have been depleted. I trotted ahead of him, turning back again and again to spur him forward, in the manner of a legitimate guide, encouraging him toward the coffee shop where traditionally we began each day.

His hands shook all the time now, and his coffee spilled frequently. His trousers and outer coat were stained beyond hope or repair.

"You ought take care of that cough," the coffee shop proprietor told him. "Go over to the clinic, they'll give you something for it. Maybe you need a shot of penicillin."

But he paid no attention. And though I could guide him capably to his usual haunts and back to our riverbank home each evening, I did not know where the clinic was or how to get him there.

I could only stay by his side, huddle close to him at night to provide him with warmth, lick his hands free of grime, and protect him from nighttime predators.

"Good boy, good boy," he would murmur to me often, the same words he had used when we met. He scratched behind my ears with his shaking fingers.

One morning — another cold day, windy and damp — he wouldn't get up, no matter how I nudged and whimpered.

"I think I'll sleep in today," he told me.

I wandered down to the river for a drink and then marked a few spots where I smelled interlopers, to remind them that this space was taken. I sat alone in the wind, feeling invigorated by it after the night in our stuffy hovel, and thought about poetry again. In my concern for Jack, I had done no composing for a long time. I began to write a poem in my mind.

O Jack, be strong, be well, my friend!

Briefly I considered the rhyming possibilities of *friend*, but the only thing that came to my mind was *end*. It was such a discouraging thought that it virtually destroyed my creativity. Demoralized, I went back to where Jack lay. His breathing was very ragged.

I tried my playful pose, rump in the air, head down and tail wagging. It was the introduction to a game we had often played, a game with complicated rules involving ownership of a filthy, much-chewed piece of rope.

He smiled but declined the invitation. "I need rest," he said, stopping to cough. "Need rest."

So I nestled by his side and stayed with him throughout the long day. He talked to me from time to time and sometimes his thoughts wandered back to the days of home and family in the past. He seemed to forget that I was there, though his fingers lay against my neck and from time to time stroked my fur.

When I had lost my mother and siblings so long before, I had felt fear and frustration but at the same time a sense of independence and adventure. Now I was older. Now I knew I could survive alone. But I had a more adult understanding of the value of companionship and what I was losing as I lay there beside my friend and felt him slip away from me.

I tried again to write a poem, an ode to Jack. Only one word kept coming to me. *Why?* I said it to myself over and over again, searching for the rhyme that would go with it and turn it into a proper elegy.

But only one word surfaced, and that was the word that concluded what would be my shortest, and saddest, poem.

Goodbye.

6

AND SO I WAS ALONE AGAIN. A pup no longer, but still awash with the yearnings of youth.

I could have curled beside Jack's body, mourning, and wasted away beside him in that grim setting. I have heard of dogs who do that out of loyalty, and are much admired for their sacrifice; they have statues and monuments erected in their honor. But such statues and monuments are always posthumous. I knew it was not what Jack would have wished for me.

"Lucky you are, and lucky you'll be!" Jack had said to me often, in better days when his spirits were high and his jug by his side.

Lucky I am! Lucky I'll be!
I wonder what's in store up ahead!

Quickly, feeling foolish, I corrected the obvious error in the poem. *In store for me,* I amended.

Poetry is a difficult art, I thought as I neatened the area where Jack still lay. It was the least I could do for him, since I had decided against wasting away in his honor.

I rubbed my head affectionately against his lifeless fingers and whimpered a goodbye, adding *why* to make it into a variation on the elegy I had composed only a few hours before. Then I turned and left the hollow under the bridge, giving a final and very ferocious growl toward the sewer pipe, in hopes of keeping the rats unnerved. As I walked away from what had been my home during almost all of my formative first year, I held my head high in homage to Jack and all that he had taught me about life, adversity, and how to obtain food.

Upright, my tail! Forward, my feet!

The next line had not yet come to me, though I was considering *fleet* as an appropriate rhyme for a leavetaking, when suddenly I spotted something that caught my attention and wrote itself into the poem:

I see a child across the street!

It was true. In this most unsavory part of the city, beside a graffiti-covered board fence, a young boy wearing an odd hat stood alone, his hands in his pockets, a captivating smile on his face. He was clearly in need of protection, though his attitude was self-confident. I suspected that he did not know what danger might come to him if he loitered here. Glancing quickly both ways, alert to the vehicles my mother had repeatedly described as my greatest enemies, and as ever on the lookout for Scar, who might be lurking almost anywhere,

I bounded across the street to the boy's side.

Panting, I looked up at him, expecting a pat of welcome on my head. Humans always reach for the head, for some reason; it is actually the spot behind each ear that we dogs most prefer to have scratched. But we tolerate the head pat until we can maneuver ourselves into a position where the human understands the need. I planned to let the boy pat my head; then I would rub myself against his legs; then he would reach down and I would tilt myself into a position so that his hand would encounter the right place. It wouldn't take long to train him. Jack had learned quickly, and this human was much younger and therefore even more educable.

To my amazement, he did not pat my head at all. He kicked me.

It wasn't a painful kick, because he was wearing sneakers that were much too large and so the toes of them were empty. In truth, it was more of a foot-nudge. But it was a surprise, and a disappointment. It was contrary to every lesson my mother had taught me about children.

"Get lost!" he said.

And that was a surprise, too. According to my education, the first words a child usually says, upon encountering a new and appealing dog (I was assuming, of course, myself to be appealing. In my new maturity, I felt that my tail, in particular, had developed a certain plumelike quality; and as for behavior, I had certainly been on my best, though I must say the boy had not), are "Can I keep him?"

So "Get lost" came as a surprise. In addition, since I already felt myself to be somewhat lost, I did not see how I could possibly "get" more so. I stared at the boy curiously. In addition to the very large shoes and the hat that looked like an unsuccessful cupcake, he was wearing enormously baggy trousers and a bright-colored shirt with writing on it.

"Beat it!" he whispered to me, appearing more frustrated than ill-tempered. "You're ruining my shot!"

Shot? He had no gun. He didn't even look like someone who *wanted* to have a gun. He was a boy. A *kid.*

I hesitated, looking around to see what was going on.

Farther down the street I saw a number of people grouped around a large camera. A tall woman with a notebook was writing things down as if they were important. A man was adjusting some tall lights with pale umbrellas behind them.

"What's with the dog?" the woman asked, looking up from her notebook. "Whose is he? Is that your dog, Willy?"

"Moi?" A thin man wearing a denim jacket asked. "No way. I'm a cat person."

Whose is he was a phrase that raised my hackles. Why is it that humans feel dogs belong to them? How can that be? Jack never felt that way, or treated me like property. We had chosen each other, Jack and I.

If I were ready to choose another human — and I was not — it would not be this thin man who had already announced his preference for cats, a dubious species at best.

Even as I was thinking about it, the man named Willy jogged toward me, carrying a leather case. "I'm just going to touch up your hair," he said cheerfully, and took a comb from the case. I winced. I didn't want my fur tampered with, and especially not by a man whose clearly professed commitment was to cats.

But he was talking, it appeared, to the boy. He removed the hat, combed and arranged the boy's hair so that it appeared windblown and casual, and then replaced the unattractive hat so that the freshly groomed hair was hidden.

"I can't get the dog to go away," the boy complained to him.

"What about the dog?" the hair person called to the camera people. "I don't want to be the one to drag him away. He looks like a biter to me!"

The dog: a phrase I loathe. A biter indeed. I wished Jack were alive. Jack would tell them where to go. There had been times in our past, Jack's and mine, when people had been apprehensive about "the dog" and Jack had been very firm with them, explaining that the dog had feelings and intelligence, that the dog had more integrity than most humans, and that, most important, the dog had a name and should be addressed accordingly. Sometimes people would drop money into Jack's outstretched hand and hurry away quickly, just to flee the lecture about man's best friend.

"I love the dog," the woman with the notebook called. "Keep the dog. The dog *works*."

I wasn't entirely certain what she meant by that. Of course I worked. I worked at staying alive, finding food, guarding against rats, and tending Jack when things turned bad.

"I'd like the dog's hair a little more disheveled, Willy," she called. "Think you can do that for me?"

Willy was the man with the comb, the one who had called me a biter. He glanced down at me now, and I raised my lip a little. I murmured a warning. It wasn't a growl, really, but Willy didn't know that.

"I only do humans," Willy announced. "Absolutely no canines. For canines you get a groomer."

I lay down as they argued. By now I wished I had simply moved on and left these humans to their unfathomable tasks. But I was beginning to sense that there could be some rewards in this for me.

"All right, places! Take your places!" The man behind the camera called, after the arguments seemed to die down a bit.

"Let's get this done while we still have the light!"

"Andrew, hit that pose again!" he called, and the boy went back to the stance I had seen at first, the grinning, self-confident pose that had attracted me from across the street.

I stood back up, alert now. My ears went taut. My tail was a fringed banner behind me.

> Beside the boy I stand! I pose!
> Erect, my ears! Shine, my nose!

"Great!" the photographer called. "Good dog! Stay!"

So I stayed. It was a new beginning for me.

7

When they finally finished taking photographs, everyone seemed to disperse quickly. Willy, the man with the
comb, snapped his makeup case closed and got into a waiting
car. The woman with the notebook snapped it shut and got
into the car with Willy.

Several other, minor people hailed passing cabs and disappeared into the traffic.

The boy, the one I had thought so briefly would become
the child I had wanted, snapped his smile off as soon as the
camera closed down. His face became a frown, and he walked
briskly off to a car with two adults who seemed to be his at-

tendants. He never looked back at me. So much for my "boy and his dog" fantasy.

I had been told "Stay" and so I stayed, partly out of curiosity and partly because I did not know what else to do.

Then only the photographer was left. It had taken him a while to fold his complicated lights, replace his equipment in cases, and load everything into a Jeep that was parked nearby. I was impressed by his meticulousness.

Finally he looked around to see if he had forgotten anything. He picked up an empty film canister and tossed it into a trash can. Then his eyes fell on me.

I was still in my "stay" position: alert, waiting, head high.

The photographer smiled. He came over, squatted beside me, and scratched behind my ear, completely bypassing the uncomfortable head pats that dogs ordinarily have to endure on short acquaintance. Clearly he was a man accustomed to dogs. My heart beat faster.

"What's up, pal?" he asked. I noted the name change. So I was Lucky no longer. It required a quick adjustment in my thinking.

Lucky I was, now I'll be Pal!

I was still pondering the second line (possibly something referring to morale, I thought) when he rose, stretched, grinned, and said the word that I most longed to hear.

"Come," the photographer said.

I followed him eagerly to the Jeep and hopped onto the back seat when he opened the door. I sat politely, avoiding making pawmarks on the seat, and tried not to lean too close to the window, though I was wild with curiosity and excitement. I had never been in a vehicle before. But there is some primal inborn awareness in dogs, and I knew instinctively that

it would not serve my future well if today I got drool and dog breath on the windows.

If he learned to love me now, I could slobber all over soon. The combination of timing, self-restraint, and discretion is the art that separates the successful dog from those foolish canines who find themselves at the ends of leashes and on the floor of school gyms having obedience lessons.

Watching carefully through the windows of the Jeep, I could see that we were making our way through the same streets that I had walked with Jack. I saw the same corner, in fact, where I had met Jack while fleeing the scar-faced dog who had beaten me out for the McDonald's breakfast and become my mortal enemy. I felt as if there should be some memorial there, a marker for Jack, whose life had been lived on that corner; but it was simply an unacknowledged place with a trash can, a mailbox, and a lamppost: nothing physical to mark a spot where the groundstone of a relationship had been laid.

As we slowed for a light, I saw suddenly the carved wooden door, with the menu attached to its window, that was the familiar entrance to Toujours Cuisine. I realized that we were passing the alley where I had been born. Eagerly I rose to the full length of my legs, unsteady on the slick surface of the car seat. I leaned toward the window, forgetting the dangers of spit on the pane, and found myself whimpering.

The photographer slowed the Jeep and turned to me with a concerned look. "You okay?" he asked. "Not carsick?"

I gave him what I thought was an imploring look. *If only,* the look said, *if only we could stop for a moment? Please? And perhaps I might find my beloved mother still on these familiar sidewalks. Or my siblings — well, really only the one, my favorite, my sister, little Wispy?*

He smiled at me. His smile was warm, intelligent, and compassionate. But he had not understood my look, or my yearning; when the light changed, he propelled the Jeep ahead. "Almost home, pal," he said consolingly.

So I lay back down on the seat and composed a mournful poem — I believe it could rightly be called an elegy — in my head. For the first time, the rhyme came easily, naturally. For the first time I felt what true poets must feel when the words fall into place.

> *Be brave, my heart; be still, be calm!*
> *Adieu to Jack. To Wisp. To Mom . . .*

My life seemed an unending series of leavetakings. Unaware of my grief and loneliness, the photographer drove around a corner, and behind us the familiar neighborhood slid away with whatever it still contained of my past.

To my surprise (and, I confess, to my chagrin, since I had just composed such a complex ballad of goodbye), we stopped in front of a brownstone building that was no more than two blocks from my old haunts.

"This is it, pal," the photographer said as he began to unload his equipment from the Jeep. "Your new home, if you feel like it. I don't have a leash, and you're free to take off if you want. Or you can come on in and make yourself comfortable. You look hungry. Could you handle some leftover pasta? If you decide to stay, I'll buy some dogfood in the morning."

I might have been tempted to trot off around the corner, back to the old neighborhood. But like Jack, he had announced himself as a leash-free human. There would be no choke collar, no rhinestone-studded lead such as I had seen on a passing Bedlington terrier (the sight had made me avert my eyes in embarrassment). It would just be me — once Lucky, now Pal — unrestrained, with what looked like a warm and pleasant roof over my head.

And pasta. To tell the truth, it was the mention of pasta that did it.

Legs, be steady! Mouth, get ready!

I trotted behind the photographer up the stairs. From hunger and anticipation I simply dismissed the high art of poetry from my mind and turned to primitive rhyming chant instead. I murmured it under my breath up three flights of stairs:

spaghetti spaghetti spaghetti spaghetti.

Quickly and happily I settled into my new digs. There was a bit of a power struggle over sleeping places until finally, grudgingly, I agreed to sleep on a blanket folded in the corner. In return, the photographer agreed to refrain from kibbles and nourish me with pasta whenever possible.

These decisions were reached, of course, without conversation. Life would be easier for dogs if humans could comprehend our speech as we do theirs. Instead, we have to resort to pantomime and subterfuge.

I won't even bother to describe the on-or-off-the-bed struggle we endured before we came to an understanding. The ultimate compromise was this: during the night, he slept on the bed and I slept on the floor. During the day, if he was at home, I slept on the floor. If he was out of the apartment or closed away in his darkroom, as he often was, I curled up on the bed. When he returned, I got down with a great show of languid boredom, leaving pawprints which he pretended not to notice.

We postponed dealing with the issue of the couch.

It was early afternoon on the third day. "Pal?" The photographer spoke gleefully to me as he emerged from the darkroom in his apartment. "You're not gonna believe this!"

He was carrying a dripping wet photograph; while I watched, he took it over near the window and examined it in the bright light there. He whistled. Startled by the sound, I jumped a bit from the folded blanket in the corner that had been designated my space. Ordinarily when a human whistles, it means that a dog is being summoned.

But this wasn't a shrill, dog-calling sound. It was a low, extended whistle of admiration. Self-admiration, actually, since he was whistling at one of his own photographs.

I could forgive him a little self-congratulation, since I am prone to it myself. I understand the feeling of ecstasy and pride when one has accomplished something. For me it is most often a particularly fine pose, perhaps on a windy day when my fur ripples and my glorious tail is extended with its ornamental fringe parted in waves and I know that I am a magnificent sight. If I could whistle then, I would. But a dog's mouth is not configured for whistles, and so most often I simply emit a low groan of pleasure, unintelligible to humans.

"Look!" he said excitedly, and knelt beside me with the wet photograph in his hands. On his part, it was simply a gesture, since he did not truly expect me to look, or to admire his work. Humans believe (wrongly) that a dog's thoughts extend no further than the basic needs of food, shelter, and reproduction.

If they only knew what complex creatures we really are, and how deeply aesthetic our tastes!

But I was touched by his gesture, and in fact, when he thought I was simply nuzzling his hand in search of tidbits, I was actually studying the photograph very carefully.

It was one that he had taken on the day of our meeting, only three days before. I stood beside the boy, who was grinning in that supercilious way, with his hands in his pockets, displaying his baggy trousers, enormous sneakers, and macaroon-like cap, pretending that he was in love with his clothes.

My look was one of disdain. Disdain for the boy, for his clothes, for his smile, for the entire surrounding world. My lip was ever so slightly curled, my eyes half closed in boredom, my ears limp with ennui.

It was, I have to admit, a marvelously sophisticated look, one that said *attitude*. I admired it. I admired myself for creating it. Unconsciously, sitting there on my frayed blanket, the photo in front of me, I created it again on the spot, lowering my eyelids, raising my lip a micromillimeter, turning my neck an infinitesimal bit to the left.

The photographer leapt to his feet and shouted in exhilaration. Once, at the back door of Toujours Cuisine, I heard a cry of that sort. A Grand Marnier soufflé had just emerged from the oven, and the chef, overwhelmed by its height and fragrance, had cried out in the same way.

"Pal!" the photographer shouted, almost delirious with pleasure. "You did it again! Can you do it on command?" he asked.

Of course I could. I could do it whenever I wished. But *command? Pardonez-moi?* A self-respecting dog does not do things on command. On *request,* perhaps.

"What shall I call it? What command can I give?" He was talking to himself but watching me.

"I know, I know!" He knelt in front of me, looked me firmly in the eye, and said in a deep, commanding voice, "*Sneer.*"

I yawned, turned around in a carefully thought-out circle,

lay down on my blanket, and placed my head, my face impassive, on my crossed front paws. The photographer's face fell.

He sighed and stroked me behind my ear.

Finally he murmured, "Pal? *Please*. For me? Sneer."

That was more like it. A humble request carries a lot more weight than a shouted command, at least with me.

I raised my head, looked at the photographer, and sneered.

In his joy, he actually turned a somersault. It was an embarrassing display, and I am glad we were the only two beings in the room. I chuckled to myself, aware of how little training it takes to make a human perform tricks of surprising idiocy.

He hugged me. He ran to the refrigerator, brought out a cold frankfurter, dangled it before my nose, and said, "Sneer."

Again I yawned. Bribery? *Mon dieu*.

Abashed but learning, he returned the bribe to the refrigerator, stood in front of me, and asked politely once again. "Pal? Please? Sneer?"

So I sneered for him one more time; he flew into one more paroxysm of joy; and finally I licked his hand, acknowledging that we were partners and friends.

Thus my career began.

8

THE PHOTOGRAPH OF ME AND THE BOY in the collapsed muffin hat appeared publicly the next week, in a Sunday supplement called "Fashions of the Times." Both of us, the photographer and I, admired it extensively. He left the publication on the coffee table, open to that page, just in case any neighbors dropped by.

Late that morning I was lying on the floor, eating some leftover lasagna while the photographer, wearing his fuzzy bathrobe, worked on the crossword puzzle and sipped coffee. The telephone rang.

"Yes," I heard him say, "he's my own dog. What breed?" He glanced over at me.

I tossed my head and yawned. *What breed.* As if it made the slightest difference. It is a shallow human indeed who actually believes that the flowing, silky hair and disdainful face of an Afghan make it a more aristocratic dog than, say, a tricolored shepherd fathered in the Outback by a roaming herding dog with a few minutes to dally. The distinction of a dog lies entirely in its innate character and intelligence, coupled with the early training of a diligent mother. I would match my wits and virtue against a best-of-show anytime. And my tail, too.

Fortunately the photographer appeared to share my view. He winked at me, an odd human habit that I have learned to appreciate but have never truly understood. Then he shrugged, and said into the receiver, "Mixed. He's a unique mix."

Unique. A pleasant word. In my mind, I coupled it with others like *physique* and *sleek.*

A second caller asked my name and age. "Pal," the photographer replied. "His name is Pal. And he's, ah, young." He looked at me and raised an eyebrow. I raised an eyebrow back. I had no idea how old I was. Almost two, perhaps? Dogs' ages are measured strangely, anyway. I think I was sort of a teenager. But *young* sounded acceptable to me.

Some of the calls were inquiring about my fee.

Fee? Dogs are not accustomed to being paid. Watchdogs generally do it for nothing more than the satisfaction of guarding turf, or for the sheer arrogant gratification that comes from terrorizing humans. Although I felt no territorial urge and had no wish to frighten anyone, I had been a sort of watchdog in the nights with Jack. I had been a protector, and would be so again for anyone I loved. But I would ask no pay for simply following the instincts of my heart.

Guide dogs are not paid. Their motives are completely benevolent, and they find joy in shepherding their humans across busy streets, avoiding honking traffic. I had taken great pride in guiding Jack during those last weeks, when his frailty had made him needy. There is no fee for such devotion.

Hunting dogs ask no compensation for pointing to a grouse concealed in foliage. The admiration they receive for the nobility and precision of their pose is compensation enough.

And simple house pets find their complete reward in simply lying at someone's feet, being scratched, ruffled, and fed, chasing a ball from time to time and looking adoringly at a human. Money can't replace that kind of contentment.

I viewed myself as something of a combination of the various categories. Though never trained as a watchdog, I had guarded Jack's turf with authority, I felt; and though untrained as a guide, I had steered and directed him in his last weeks with patience and gentleness. I had little interest in hunting as a sport or game as a meal, but I could say of myself that I was adroit at the pose, and that my glorious tail would, if called upon, lend itself to the kind of vigilant stance that looks fine on a fall morning in the woods. Certainly, more than anything, I enjoyed being a pet.

But not for pay.

Curious, I listened to the photographer say that my fee was high. "Pricey," he said to the callers who were inquiring. "I'm afraid he's a pricey model."

That seemed to pique their interest, and they asked about my availability.

"Next Thursday?" I heard him say. "Well, I'll check my calendar . . ."

I woofed politely from my blanket and licked a bit of tomato sauce from my lip.

"I mean, *his* calendar," the photographer amended. "He's very much in demand."

Of course I wasn't, not then. I had posed once, sneered once, appeared in a newspaper supplement once, and that was all.

But before long I *was* in demand. Everyone who called wanted to book me for what they referred to as a "shoot."

I didn't like the sound of it. But the photographer, sensing my discomfort, stroked me behind my left ear and explained that it had nothing to do with firearms; it was a photo shoot.

"All you have to do is stand there and sneer," he explained, "and I'll get rich."

I raised my eyebrow at him.

"We," he corrected. "*We'll* get rich. Famous, too," he added cheerfully.

He closed up the newspaper, leaving the crossword puzzle undone, rinsed his coffee cup, and looked thoughtfully at me.

"Know what, Pal?" he said. "I'm going to have to give you a bath."

There are, I suppose, various and unique ways to ruin a Sunday afternoon. But this proved to be the worst. Never in my entire existence had I had a bath. My mother, when I was a pup, licked me clean often enough, sometimes quite roughly. Once I had played in a mud puddle near our alley home, and although I shook myself ferociously afterward, sending dirty water flying everywhere, my mother had nonetheless cleaned me endlessly, scolding all the while and warning my brothers and sister about the obvious damage a puddle could do to one's appearance.

Then I had lived for a long time with Jack. Jack and I did not take baths. The river, our only water source, was coated with yellow foam and did not lend itself to missions of personal hygiene. And it was a kind of badge of honor, I think, for Jack and me, that even encrusted with grime as we were, we maintained our dignity at all times.

Jack had confided once, chuckling, that one damp morning he had found a mushroom growing out of his shoe, at the place where the sole separated from the upper leather and had mildewed.

I was sorry that our language barrier prevented me from describing the mushroom to the photographer that morning. Fond as he was of Italian sauces on his pastas, I thought perhaps the possibility of homegrown mushrooms might have steered him away from his determined course toward a bath.

When I heard him filling the bathtub, I tiptoed silently into the bedroom and flattened my body until I was able, though uncomfortably, to slither under the bed.

"Pal?" I heard him calling. But I stayed silent and hidden.

"Pal?" He called again, and he was using a kind of falsely sweet tone, a pseudo-friendly voice. I disregarded it.

> *O silently, stealthily, safe in my lair!*
> *If only —*

As happens so often, I had not completed my couplet because I was searching for the perfect concluding rhyme. I was toying with the word *debonair,* or perhaps even the wonderful phrase *devil-may-care,* and how it could apply. But my usual problem — lack of awareness of my tail's whereabouts — betrayed me.

"Gotcha!" the photographer exclaimed. He grabbed the tip of my tail where it extended from the underside of the bed. From there it was just a brief and painful moment of tugging, and I was caught.

I submitted grudgingly to the indignity of it. I sat in a half-full bathtub and allowed him to rub dog shampoo into my fur. I gritted my teeth and kept my poise as he poured buckets of rinse water over me. I permitted him to wrap and rub me with a thick towel. Finally I let him aim a hair dryer at me for a few warm and terrifying moments and then scrape at me with a steel comb.

But I did not let him buckle the leather collar that he had somehow slipped around my neck. When he suggested it, I glittered my eyes and growled. The photographer was gracious in admitting defeat.

"Actually," he said, "I think it enhances your look, that primitive nakedness. We'll leave it as is. Good idea, Pal."

As if it were *his*, the idea. Ha. But he put the collar away in a drawer.

Before long the calendar was full, and my price, apparently, had risen. I watched as the photographer opened envelopes that contained checks, and heard him chortle with satisfaction as he put them away. He and I were busy every day, driving in the Jeep from location to location. It wasn't difficult work. For the *Vogue* shoot, I stood on the steps of the stock exchange beside a skinny woman wearing a long, billowing gown. When the photographer gave me the signal, I sneered and the camera clicked.

For a Calvin Klein ad, I posed, sneering, beside a man wearing nothing but a plaid towel and a bored look.

On the cover of *Gourmet*, I sneered at a picnic lunch on a Tuscan hillside. I sneered wearing a milk mustache in several publications and eventually on a billboard as well, and in *Vanity Fair* I sneered at a group of *paparazzi* blocking my path to a showing at the Cannes Film Festival.

I became a world traveler, adroit in airports and taxis, and added some Italian to the French I had understood since infancy.

I sneered at Paul Newman's salad dressing, raising millions for charity. I did a dogfood commercial, sneering at the competitor's product and then wolfing down a bowl (and oh, it was difficult) of crunchy liver-flavored nuggets. I sneered at Senator Strom Thurmond on a political poster. I sneered on the Jay Leno show, seated on a couch beside Cybill Shepherd, who tried to sneer back but collapsed instead in giggles, causing the shoulder straps of her silk dress to slip.

I did a calendar but turned down a guest appearance on *Oprah*. I declined to do an autobiography, though publishers called almost daily, offering the services of the most distinguished ghostwriters.

I began, of course, to have imitators. There was a German shepherd who could produce a voluptuous yawn on request, but it did not have the panache of my sneer. A matched pair of Pomeranians who could raise their upper lips in unison appeared on Dave Letterman's show but did not garner much praise or any further bookings. In truth, they were laughable.

The photographer and I stayed up late that evening to watch them, but we went to bed satisfied that they were no more than a poor joke.

My frayed blanket, so permeated with my own history and scent, disappeared. I was upgraded to a dog bed filled with cedar shavings from L. L. Bean: a costly and impressive sleeping place but one that filled me with loathing. Toward the end of our first year together, the photographer and I moved from the shabby apartment to a fancier neighborhood three blocks away, into a seven-room, eighth-floor co-op with a river view, so that now, standing on the balcony, I looked down upon my own past. The apartment was decorated with a southwestern motif, with weavings and pottery everywhere and on the floor an assortment of costly Navajo rugs which I was directed to avoid walking upon. Everything smelled new and expensive and clean and completely without pungence or charm.

The photographer hired someone to walk me, because his life had become so busy with social engagements now that he was rich and famous.

The dogwalker, an unemployed actor, was a pleasant enough person but not at all sympathetic to my needs. He insisted on using a leash. I began to think seriously about running away.

9

I THINK IT IS FAIR TO SAY THAT I WAS, and am, a clever dog. I had always, since infancy, been able to think my way through problems that confronted me.

I have heard that there is a book that rates dog breeds according to intelligence. It is a book, I'm told, that makes poodle owners very happy and Afghan owners fall into severe states of depression.

But I question its accuracy. One of its testing procedures — so I have been told — involves placing a towel over the head of one's dog and then observing how quickly the dog wriggles free of the towel.

What kind of test is that? It fails to consider various important factors.

For example, if I happened to be lying on my bed of cedar shavings late some evening, and in the same room (this has happened) the photographer was entertaining a large group of friends by playing irritating music too loudly, and if several of his friends (this has happened) were smoking cigarettes, filling the room with a completely repellent haze of gray smoke; and if, under those circumstances, someone happened to drop a towel on my head?

According to the book, I would be deemed "highly intelligent" if I removed the towel. *Pardonez-moi?*

I don't think so. I think any highly intelligent, self-respecting dog, poodle, Afghan, dingo, or coyote, would be grateful for that towel, and would heave a sigh of relief and go peacefully to sleep.

I, of course, being of mixed ancestry, am not listed in that book. But I feel certain that I am a clever dog, able to discern when and when not to allow a towel to remain on my head.

Yet somehow I was not able to work out a foolproof plan for running away. My life had become so organized and so protected that I had no moments for wandering on my own. There was no way that I could simply, casually, disappear.

I could have, in my days with Jack. Often during our time on the street I would go for a stroll. I had physical needs to attend to, after all; Jack understood that. Sometimes I wandered out of his line of vision, turning the corner, simply checking the neighborhood. In truth, I was always on the lookout for two things: the appearance of Scar, so that I could flee (later, as I developed more self-confidence, I began to think that instead of fleeing I might fight), or the appearance of my lost sister, Wispy, who I always hoped might be somewhere just around the corner, looking for me.

Occasionally I glimpsed Scar. He was usually lurking some distance away, not noticing me, so that I was never called upon to make the crucial decision between fleeing and fighting. I would watch from my safe stance as he terrorized some other puppy or human. Our last confrontation had been indecisive, and I knew I must one day face him again. In those last days with Jack, my attention had been solely directed to my friend. It had not been a time for battle. But I had vowed that when the time was right, I would drive Scar from the neighborhood forever.

I had composed a valiant little ode that I murmured to myself whenever I saw my mortal enemy. It made me feel strong while safely postponing any real dangerous action.

I vow this, Scar, with all my might!
Someday I'll beat you in a fight!

It was a silly little couplet, and I thought I could do better; I wanted, actually, to try to rhyme the word *confrontation*, now that I had a greater and more sophisticated command of language. But I simply hadn't gotten around to it yet; I'd been so busy with my career.

As for Wispy, and my search, I simply repeated as a little talisman

Wispy, sister, hear my rhyme —
I'll seek you till the end of time!

(I had originally composed *till the end of my life*, which I felt was more truthful and accurate, but as a poem it was simply too amateurish.) I had some small hope that my repetition of the verse might magically cause her to reappear someday. But in my wanderings during those months with Jack, there was never the slightest glimpse. Sometimes I would see a little female who reminded me of my sister, but on close examination, on an exchange of sniffs, there was only disappointment and the awareness that the world was very full of little crossbreed females with mottled fur and inadequate, crooked tails.

I always returned to Jack after a stroll. I had no inclination to stray from the place of greatest comfort and camaraderie.

Similarly, in the early days with the photographer, there were countless opportunities for me to run off. There were no leash, no cage, no conditions. I remained because he was kind, because he fed me pasta, and because his plaid bathrobe had a pungent and agreeable smell.

Now things had changed. Now the dog walker had a hideous retractable leash, which of course required that a collar be placed around my neck. The photographer had a new cashmere bathrobe, which made me sneeze, and shared pasta seemed a thing of the past. Now I was famous and rich, and my food was served to me in a Santa Fe pottery bowl that was embellished with my name, PAL, on its side. But I no longer had the freedom to walk away.

During the day, when I was working at various locations, there were always guards, off-duty policemen hired to hold back the crowds who waved and whistled at me. The Jeep was a thing of the past, relegated to the garage, and I was whisked from spot to spot by limo. While the photographer talked business on the cell phone, I pressed my nose sadly against the tinted glass, no longer worried about the smears, only longing for a life beyond the confines of what my own had become.

At each new location I would be collared, leashed, and led to a place where I was told to attend to my bodily needs. Sometimes a bowl of water would be brought, or a dry-tasting biscuit would be handed to me by one of the assistants. Then I would be led to my spot at the side of a thin person — sometimes male, sometimes female, sometimes apparently neuter — in new-smelling clothes. My leash and collar would be unclipped, and someone would say sharply, "Sit. Stay." If, restlessly, I shifted positions or turned my head, the sharp voice would command me again, and there would be a veiled threat in the tone. No one called me by name.

Once again I had become "The Dog."

I no longer took pride in my pose or my sneer. I simply did my job, watching fruitlessly for some unattended moment when I could simply walk away.

It came, finally, on a spring day when we were shooting a commercial for antihistamine tablets. We were assembled on a golf course quite far from the city. We had been more than an hour in the limo: time for the photographer to make four lengthy phone calls and read the entire *Wall Street Journal*.

The script called for me ("The Dog") to sit at the edge of the green, watching attentively as two golfers wearing baggy trousers on their legs and visors on their heads attempted to hit the ball a few inches into the cup. Each one, interrupted by a sneeze, would miss. The crowd (forty people hired to stand around the green wearing light-colored clothes and animated facial expressions) would send up a groan at each miss. Then, as the failed and allergic golfers looked on in dismay, handkerchiefs to their noses, The Dog was to walk over and nudge the ball into the cup. Then I was to sit there and sneer at the camera while the crowd cheered.

It made absolutely no sense, and I have no idea why they

thought it would sell antihistamine tablets. But they were paying the photographer a huge sum of money for the use of The Dog, and to me, it was just one more job in my increasingly lethargic life.

I hadn't composed a poem in weeks.

Then, suddenly, as I sat at the edge of the green, looking theatrically alert and interested (despite my total boredom), there was an alarming clap of thunder. A few drops of rain fell. The golfers looked up, confused. I could see the photographer cover his camera quickly, to protect the lens.

The sky darkened and a lightning bolt outlined a jagged streak at the horizon. The hired crowd, feeling heavier raindrops, headed for the cover of the trees.

I sat and looked as I had been instructed: alert, interested. In truth, I *was* becoming more and more interested as I saw that everyone was dispersing and that they were forgetting The Dog.

The photographer was packing his equipment very hastily into cases. The two actors who were playing the roles of the golfers ran to a car.

"Get away from the trees!" someone yelled. "It's dangerous under the trees!"

Someone else yelled, "It's dangerous out in the open!"

Another crack of thunder, much louder, and a streak of lightning, much closer, sent everyone scattering chaotically. I heard shouts, rain, thunder, and cars starting. But I did not hear anyone say "Come!" in the sort of commanding voice that alerts you to the fact that they are calling a dog.

So I simply walked away. My walk was casual at first, for I expected at any second to hear the familiar "Come!" But after a moment I began to trot. Then, gradually sensing my freedom, I stretched my legs into a liberating lope. In a mo-

ment I had traversed the fourteenth fairway, jumped a fence, and found myself completely alone, running with blissful abandon down a country road through a rainstorm.

I was thoroughly wet and exquisitely happy. My magnificent tail, profuse even when dripping, flowed behind me.

I'm free I'm free I'm free I'm free!

To which there was only one obvious second line:

I'm me I'm me I'm me I'm me!

Poetry had returned.

10

"Can I keep him?"

There. That was what a child was *supposed* to say when a dog followed him home.

Or her. This child was a girl, actually.

I had found her (she thought she had found me, but the reverse was actually true) after roaming the countryside for two days and nights. At first I had wandered joyfully, feeling myself to be a truly free and untamed creature, sharing my world with deer, raccoons, hawks, and countless other inhabitants of the outdoors.

But after two days I realized I was having difficulty with the food. My first cuisine had been French, as I was weaned from mother's milk to the world of pâtés and terrines and gâteaux. I knew a béchamel sauce from a Hollandaise, and the difference mattered to me. My early poetry had had a Gallic influence; remember *"Adieu to Jack . . ."*? Not a mature work, of course, but one that played with bilingualism.

My stay with Jack, though never in the least luxurious, had nonetheless had a certain standard as far as food was concerned. Sorting through discarded garbage after the market had closed, Jack had carefully carved away spoilage from apples and pears with his penknife. He had examined each morsel carefully before slicing it into portions for himself and me. Jack was a fastidious man, though hard times had caused him to be less selective than he might once have been.

It was while sharing discarded pizza remains that Jack had first alerted me to the delights of Italian cuisine.

"This isn't bad, Lucky," he had said (for I was still Lucky then), "but wait till you taste a real good pasta. Maybe a linguini with clam sauce, or a fettucini Alfredo. Then you'll know what Italian cooking's all about."

And so I had, through the photographer, before our life was ruined by fame and fortune. Oh, the *puttanesca* sauce! The *funghi* and the *carbonara!*

Dogs don't weep, but the memory of those sauces, French and Italian both, almost brought tears to my canine eyes during those two days in the woods. I thought of tender asparagus — perhaps a *crème d'asperges vertes* — when I found myself, ravenous, nibbling at slimy swamp cabbage; and when I shared a rotting rabbit carcass with a roaming possum, I remembered *lapin au saupiquet* with ineffable sadness.

It was, in fact, while gnawing at rabbit that I remembered watching Scar devour rat remains, and the disgust I had felt at the time. Suddenly I felt with horror that I had been re-

80

duced to a creature as primitive as my enemy, and I resolved to turn my life around once again.

Those two days had taught me that I was not cut out for a survivalist existence. The romance of it was false. Carefully I found my way back to a road. I shook myself to rid my fur of the reek of rotting *lapin*, took a deep breath, and set out at a trot to seek a more amenable life somewhere.

It was not very long before I saw the little girl, who was carrying schoolbooks and just turning into a curving dirt driveway that led to a small brick farmhouse covered with ivy. Obviously well brought up, she spoke softly in greeting and held her hand out politely for me to sniff. Then, gently, she stroked my head and neck. I moved my lovely tail back and forth for her to admire.

She had a similar tail of hair at the back of her head, and she swung hers back and forth in reply. I looked at it carefully, assessing it as a rival tail. But human tails do not compare with those of dogs. Hers was tied rather messily with a band of ribbon, and there was something that looked like a wad of chewing gum near the end. I do have to deal with burrs and other intrusions from time to time, so I understood the problem. Still, it did not appear that she had even tried to gnaw it loose.

When she smiled at me, I saw that her front teeth were missing, which obviously accounted for her failure in adequate grooming. Perhaps she had been in a terrible fight.

Thinking of battles reminded me of Scar, my enemy, and I glanced apprehensively around. But I was far from the city now. Scar was in my past, both geographically and chronologically. Alas, I thought sadly, so was Wispy.

The little girl invited me to walk beside her, and I stayed obediently at her heels as she continued the length of the driveway and opened the back door of the house. By her side I entered the kitchen.

"He followed me home," she told her mother.

"Really?" her mother replied skeptically, and looked down at me. I sat very still, using my best posture: cocked head, arched neck, attentive look. I flicked my tail to the side, hoping it was in a flowing, silky state. I tried to arrange it into a question-mark shape, but as you know, we dogs do not have as much control as we would like over our tails.

"Can I keep him?"

Her mother chuckled. "I'm sure he belongs to someone."

"He doesn't have a collar."

"Well, he must have lost it. We'll have to try to find his owner. Actually," she said, leaning down to look at me more closely, "he looks familiar." She patted my head and peered into my face. I liked her pat and her smell — she was without perfume but had a little cake batter on her fingers — but I feared her perceptions. I knew why she found me familiar. She had seen me sneering on magazine covers, billboards, and TV commercials. It would only be a matter of time before she remembered that.

I arranged my lips in something of a smile, wanting no hint of the famous expression to betray my identity. Fragments of a desperate little poem began in my mind.

Smile, lips! Hide, sneer!

I was running through the possible rhymes (there were some spectacular ones — *souvenir, pioneer, chandelier* — but in truth I thought using *fear* would reflect my feelings more accurately) but had not yet completed the couplet to my poetic satisfaction when my creativity was interrupted by the placement of a glass bowl near my feet. Then, beside it, a second. One was a bowl of water, and the other appeared, to my amazement, to be *boeuf bourguignon*. I touched my tongue to it in rapture.

"Leftover stew," the girl's mother explained to me in a soft voice. Turning to the girl, she said, laughing, "Hope he likes mushrooms, Emily!"

Ah, if she only knew my history. *Champignons!* They had been among my first and favorite solid foods. My brothers had disdained the delicate little morsels, but Wispy and I had tasted them with delight, and Mother had been pleased at our discernment.

Daintily I nudged the mushrooms out of the stew with my tongue and nibbled them one by one with appreciation. Then I consumed the remaining beef and gravy, even eating the carrots — not my favorite vegetables — with enthusiasm. I followed lunch with a long drink of water from the companion bowl. Surely a good *boeuf bourguignon* is second only to a fine *spaghetti bolognese;* at least, that is my opinion.

I tried to remember the polite way to inquire about the location of the facilities. Living in the woods, it had not been a matter of importance. Living with the photographer, I had been taken outdoors, to curbside, twice a day. And in my days with Jack, we had each morning shared companionably the amenities of the river and its banks.

I walked with dignity to the door and stood beside it with a questioning look. *Avoid the sneer,* I repeated to myself. *At any cost, do not sneer.*

"He wants to go out, Emily. Open the door for him." The mother was mixing her cake batter again.

"But what if he runs away?" the little girl asked in a tremulous voice.

I laughed inwardly, but the mother echoed my laughter aloud. "Why on earth would he run away, Emily, when he has just been fed a bowl of beef stew?" Ah, a woman who understood me completely. My heart leapt.

Emily let me out and I investigated the bushes with their various smells. No dogs lived here. That was good. I wasn't ready for a territorial battle.

However, I perceived that there were cats. I sniffed Cat — that distinctive, oily, pungent odor, quite disagreeable to a dog — everywhere. That could be a bore, dealing with cats. But I decided on the basis of the stew, the child, the kind voice of the woman, and the fact that I was exhausted after two days and nights of wilderness adventure that I could compromise on the cat issue. Carefully I lifted my leg against the thick leaves of an evergreen *Raphiolepsis*, relieved myself, and marked this place as mine.

Then I went back and scratched politely on the door of the house where my new family was waiting.

11

THERE DIDN'T SEEM TO BE A FATHER. My new family resembled, in that way, a dog's family: the mother, caring attentively for the young, and the father long gone. I did not want to reflect too deeply on the failure of my own beloved mother to stay with her offspring, the way Emily's mother obviously had. It was simply the way of dogs. I had to remember that.

Unlike a dog's family, there was no litter. The little girl, Emily, seemed to be the only child. Charmingly, she showed me around the house, pointing out the most comfortable places. There was a corner in the hall where sunlight from the window warmed the wood floor to just the right temperature. I lay there for a moment, curled in a semicircle, testing the spot, and almost drifted off to sleep, still exhausted from my time in the woods. But Emily urged me up to look around some more.

"See, here's a fireplace!" she said, leading me into the living room. "In the winter we have a fire here, and it smells wonderful. You could —"

She was pointing to the hooked rug in front of the hearth, indicating that I could doze there before the fire. It created a very inviting picture in my mind, something worthy of a calendar: "By the Fireside," or some such domestic title. The image was less sophisticated than my previous calendar work, for which I had mustered a sneer for each month (December had me sneering at Santa's Workshop — imagine), and I found the quiet domestic scene infinitely more appealing.

But I continued to smell cats. It was unnerving. I glanced apprehensively around the living room. Something mounded and dark on a chair caught my attention, but on closer examination I could see that it was simply a folded sweater.

> *Alert, my nose! Be watchful, eyes!*
> *Don't let —*

I was working on the next line, planning to use *surprise* as the rhyme at the end. But again Emily urged me on. She was eager for me to see everything.

"Come on," she said, and pranced toward the stairs. "I'll show you my room, and you can see Bert and Ernie. They're on my bed."

Padding up the narrow staircase behind her, I gave a little inward dog-chuckle. It is a thing that dogs have in common with human young: the love of, the *need* of, stuffed animals to carry about, tussle with, and sleep beside. The photographer, in what I was already beginning to think of as my previous life, had provided me with various sheepskin toys: a fleecy bone, a human form, and a ball. I had licked and worried them into dingy disrepair, but I had missed them during my days in the woods, and I missed them now.

Maybe, I thought, Emily would let me have one of hers: Bert, perhaps, or Ernie. I knew them both from television. They were goofy-faced and garishly colored, not as satisfying as the sheepskins of my past, but I knew that they would be soft and chewable. I had seen some stuffed Berts and Ernies while I was doing a Toys "R" Us commercial once.

She led me down a pleasant hallway, and I followed her trustingly when she turned into a bedroom thickly carpeted and filled with books and toys.

"Look, Bert! Look, Ernie!" she chirped. "This is our new dog! He doesn't have a name yet, but —"

I froze. The two mounds of fur heaped on her bed near the pillows froze as well. Two sets of pale, hostile eyes glittered, reminding me of my frightening nights among the hordes of rats. But even as the cats (Siamese, the absolute worst for a dog) remained motionless, they began to swell. Their bodies enlarged as Emily and I watched, and they began, in unison, to make a terrifying sound. It was a low and ominous growl. Their eyes did not leave me for an instant.

I, too, am capable of growling. But my growl would have been nothing compared to the ferocity of theirs. It would have been a pathetic joke. So I remained mute. I tried to think, through my panic, what to do.

Somehow, throughout my life to this point, I had lived under the protection of humans and had never faced grave danger. The only similar situations in my memory were the confrontations with Scar so long ago. What had saved me the

87

first time, when I was still just a pup, was my intuitive knowledge of how to address a superior when the odds were against me. The second time, the battle in the night, I was fortified in courage by the need to protect Jack; even then, it had been not a victory but a draw, from which I emerged bleeding.

Now I was faced again with a fearful enemy — a pair, actually, of enemies — and I could draw no courage from the need to protect the little girl. She was merrily prancing about the room, unafraid, chattering to the growling creatures whose attention was entirely focused on me.

Shameful though it is to admit it, the odds were against me, even though I was fully grown and had led a successful and financially lucrative life. There were two of them, and one of me. They were cats, and I am a dog.

Carefully, moving slowly so that they didn't take my movement as a threat, I lowered my body to the floor. Then, still in slow motion, I rolled over to my back and exposed my belly to the beasts.

This is the way a dog admits defeat. It was degrading. But it was absolutely necessary in order to survive, caught as I was in a small room with two predators.

Frantically, I tried to create a conciliatory poem that I might present to them as a kind of homage, acknowledging their superiority, so that they would allow me to live.

> *Noble felines! O beasts supreme!*
> *I hold you in . . . ah . . . extreme esteem.*

It wasn't good. I floundered, trying to find the words in rhyme to notify them of my clear inferiority and my desperate desire to survive. It was difficult to compose lying on my back; I had not attempted it before.

They didn't seem to be listening anyway.

To my amazement, the child, Emily, walked over to the bed where the wild creatures lay poised for attack. I watched her, looking upside-down from my abject, humiliating posture on the rug, with my legs waving in the air and my tail a useless appendage beneath me.

"You silly old things," Emily said in her sweet voice. To my horror, she reached out her hand. She was within biting range of their alarming fangs.

"He's just a dog," she explained, stroking them one by one. Still embarrassingly upended, I watched as their fur shrank to its previous sleek size. Their eyes closed. Their growls changed in tone and became reverberating purrs of contentment.

Since no one had been listening anyway, I gave my poem some thought and presented a revised version, emphasizing my appreciation of the cats but alerting them as well to my own stature, certainly equal if not more than that.

> *Fur so fine! Eyes agleam!*
> *You rival me in self-esteem!*

I righted my body and stood again, hoping that perhaps no one had noticed those few moments when I had prostrated myself in such a debasing way. I wiggled a bit and then rubbed my back against the side of the bed, pretending that something was caught in my fur, that I itched and therefore had briefly found it necessary to lie upside-down on the rug.

"Come say hello to Bert and Ernie," Emily suggested. She was sitting beside them on the bed, still stroking their throats; they had both arched their necks in a way that looked luxurious and self-indulgent. They ignored me completely.

Warily, I leaned forward and touched my nose first to Bert, then to Ernie. Then I stood back, aloof, and yawned.

A good yawn, precisely timed, says it all, I think.

12

AND SO I TOOK UP RESIDENCE in a house with cats. We co-existed. Bert and Ernie were reserved rather than unfriendly. I never heard them growl again, and realized that their apparent hostility at our meeting resulted from the surprise of it. We conversed from time to time, but their voices had an irritating nasal quality that set my teeth on edge, and they were (like all cats) boring, self-absorbed, and somewhat malicious in their remarks. For the most part I sought my amusement elsewhere.

We ate side by side, from two bowls (for they shared one) on the kitchen floor. Theirs smelled of tuna, which repelled me, so I was not tempted to sneak a taste. And mine had no appeal for them.

Frankly, it had little appeal for me, either. It was high-quality horsemeat from a can, but I had been accustomed to pasta with a variety of sauces. I made do with the new diet but tried from time to time, when Emily and her mother dined on macaroni or tortellini, to express my interest in a dietary change. I sat politely, looking wistful and needy, beside the kitchen table while they had supper. It didn't seem to work. Emily slipped me a morsel occasionally, but her mother had no such inclination.

"If he *begged*," her mother said, "I'd send him outdoors. I can't stand a dog who begs during meals. But it's hard to scold him when he's just sitting there like that."

I was glad to overhear her, because it prevented me from indulging in that appalling behavior: lifting my paws in a supplicating way. Despite my mother's admonitions so long ago, I had actually been considering it.

"Doesn't he have a nice face?" Emily said to her mother. "He smiles all the time."

I gulped, without changing my facial expression. Emily was correct about my smile. Since arriving at their house, I had made a conscious effort to maintain a pleasant, cheerful countenance. It wasn't difficult, because in fact it was a pleasant and cheerful household, except for that brief early encounter with the cat duo.

But the truth — the real reason for my perpetual grin — was that I didn't want them to recognize me. My previous facial expression, sneering and disdainful, had become famous; back in the city, people continually stopped me on the street when I was being walked. *People* magazine had published a photograph and included a brief biography of my official dog walker, an out-of-work actor originally from Madison, Wisconsin.

Emily's mother had several times commented on how familiar I looked, how she was quite certain she had seen me before somewhere. I did not under any circumstances want her to recall *where*. So I conscientiously worked on maintaining a serene and blissful face. Dogs can do that. You see it occasionally when a dog scratches a certain place on his own side and an inadvertent smile appears. I had only to recreate that same smile and make it into a habit.

For the first weeks I was not certain whether, in fact, Emily's mother would allow me to remain. The plaintive "Can I keep him?" from a child most often brings about a no. So I felt that my tenure was uncertain. Then there began to be hints that I might stay. The bowl, for example. For a number of days they fed me from an old baking dish. But suddenly a new bowl appeared: a heavy ceramic bowl with, I am reluctant to describe, the word FIDO on its side. Heinous though the FIDO was, still, the dish was clearly a dog bowl purchased for me, an investment in my permanent residency.

Then, of course, the acquisition of a name. One cool evening after dinner, as we sat by the fire, Emily said again, "Isn't he great?"

Her mother laughed and nodded, agreeing tacitly to my greatness. Then she said, "I guess he's a keeper."

"Hey, did you hear that, Keeper?" Emily asked in delight.

It became my new name. First I had been Lucky, then Pal. Now I was to be Keeper, it seemed. Well, there are worse dog names. I had met a dachshund named Kielbasa once.

They gave it to me, I answered to it, I came when they called me by it, and I tried to live up to it. Being named Keeper meant, I felt, that my future was secure, and I began, in my spare moments, to create a small, casual poem on the subject:

Lucky I was, Pal I became!
Now, at last, Keeper . . .

The second line was giving me trouble. *Keeper's what I'm called?* Somehow it just didn't work.

Finally, the conclusive event: a license.

One evening, sitting by the fire, Emily's mother commented, "We have to get Keeper a license."

I had one already, of course. Back in the city, back in the apartment I had shared with the photographer, my small metal license tag dangled from the collar that was usually kept, along with the leash, on a hook in the kitchen. I suppose the photographer, by now, had enshrined it in some nostalgic fashion. Perhaps it was framed.

Yes, I like to think that it was framed: encased in glass, perhaps with a small engraved label saying PAL. Perhaps there would be dates, indicating my tenure. It would no doubt hang on the wall near the piano.

Thinking about it, I confess that I choked up a bit. I visualized the photographer there in the apartment, maybe with some friends over for dinner. Afterward, during coffee, someone would move to the piano and let his fingers drift into some old show tune. Then his eye would catch the newly framed memento on the wall. The label, engraved PAL. And the small license tag (perhaps bronzed now) fastened meticulously onto a piece of velvet.

The photographer would tell my story, and the pianist would play softly in the background. There would likely be moist eyes and a moment of silence.

I might, I supposed, even become the lyrics of a song.

> *Gentle Pal, O dog supreme —*
> *Where are you now? What might have been?*

Well, it didn't rhyme exactly. Maybe if I changed the first line to *"O dog so clean."* If "been" were pronounced the British way . . .

No. Maybe *"O dog, my Pal through thick or thin —"*

Well! That was it, of course. Sometimes, through careful revision, a true poet finds his way to the perfect combination of words.

"I've made an appointment with the vet," Emily's mother was saying. "He has to have a rabies shot before we can get the license."

Of course she didn't know that I had already had all my shots. But I didn't care. I'd have them again — and again and again — if it meant that I would be licensed, I would be legal, I would be *theirs*.

I bounded toward the stairs, intending to tell the news to Bert and Ernie, who would inevitably be found on Emily's bed, posing as pillows. Never the closest of buddies, we nonetheless did communicate from time to time. Pausing on the staircase, where I was still in full view of the inhabitants of the living room, Emily and her mother, I assumed a proud and regal pose, a pose of gratitude.

> *Observe the dog! He's yours! You're his!*
> *What a glorious day this is!*

They paid no attention of course, because my poetry was inaudible to humans. But Emily did glance up, saw me posing there, and smiled. So I continued up the stairs.

Bert and Ernie were, as I had known they would be, curled up together, asleep on Emily's bed. I nosed them awake. They both yawned and looked at me with sleepy impatience.

"Whaaaaat?" they asked. "What do you waaaant?" The cats had a habit of speaking in concert, and their voices were reedy whines, very unlike the assertive, imperious way a dog speaks.

"I'm to be licensed," I announced proudly, and with gruff humility.

Bert yawned again, and stretched. Ernie licked his paws fastidiously.

"Whhhhy?" they asked.

"Well, of course you wouldn't understand. *Cats* don't have to be licensed. But when a dog is chosen by a family — when a family commits itself to the lifelong care of a dog —"

Bert and Ernie looked at each other and yawned in unison. Bert began to tend his whiskers. Ernie languidly clenched and unclenched his paws, making claws appear and disappear in a shockingly exhibitionistic way. Through slitted eyes he examined each claw, assessing its beauty. It was clear that they were both jealous of me.

"— then the dog receives a license. It's a sort of public statement. An emblem," I continued, pretending not to notice that they were ignoring me out of spiteful envy.

"A license," they chorused in their smirking, pompous voices.

"I composed a poem for the occasion," I told them, and recited it dramatically.

> *Observe the dog! He's yours! You're his!*
> *What a glorious day this is!*

Bert gave a throaty chuckle. "*Poetic* license?" he suggested, and Ernie snickered.

"*Doggerel,*" Ernie commented cruelly.

Then they stretched themselves out again, entwined around each other. Their eyes became slits once more. Ignoring my presence, they went back to sleep.

Disgruntled, I returned to the living room, allowed Emily to rub behind my ears, and finally settled down, though I indulged in a few murderous fantasies about cats before I slept.

A frightening coincidence occurred when I was taken the next day to the vet. I recognized the building and the office as the same one that I had visited before, when I had been in residence with the photographer. I remembered sitting miserably on the same metal table, long ago, to receive the necessary inoculations that are part of a well-bred dog's life.

So I began, on entering the office, to tremble. My fear was not about injections, which I knew already were almost painless, but that I would be recognized. I sat huddled and shaking, but trying desperately to maintain my smile, because I knew that the changed facial expression would be my salvation. It was the much-photographed sneer that had been my hallmark. Without it, I could perhaps pass as a different dog.

I also tried to keep my unruly tail lowered, since its magnificence could give me away as well. It was not difficult, since I was nervous, and a frightened tail tends to stay limp of its own volition.

It worked. Although somewhere in the filing cabinets of that clinical setting there were records of a dog named Pal, no one made the connection. I became a whole new folder under the new name of Keeper.

Then, after Emily and her mother patted my head sympathetically, I was given a rabies shot and several others that would ensure the acquisition of a license. Sure enough, within a few days the meaningful little metal tag arrived and was clipped to a collar along with a separate tag bearing my name. For the first time I did not object to a collar. I had a home now, and a family, and the symbolic jingle-jangle of my tags reminded everyone, including the cats, of my status.

The cats winced when I walked past, pretending that their delicate ears were pained by my jingling. But I knew it was only their pride that suffered. They had no tags themselves to proclaim their standing. They resorted to sarcasm, always the weapon of lesser creatures.

"Hot diggety dog," they began to say in haughty, sarcastic voices as I jingled past. I thought it was unworthy of them and did not lower myself to give a reply.

13

TIME PASSED AND I SETTLED COMFORTABLY into the peaceful life of a child's pet and a family member. I slept on the floor beside Emily's bed and licked her face to wake her each morning, ignoring the preening and stretching of Bert and Ernie, who occupied one of the pillows.

Summer was an exquisite time. With school finished, Emily was at home each day, and together we played in the yard and explored the nearby meadows. I frisked about like a puppy, chasing butterflies and grasshoppers. Emily and I took turns hiding in the tall unmown grass and leaping out to surprise each other. Again and again I retrieved the ball that I had trained her to throw.

Now and then the pair of cats deigned to join us out of doors, but they always pretended to think that our games were boring and juvenile, and after a short romp they inevitably found a sunny spot in which to languish, yawning.

At the end of that idyllic summer, Emily's front teeth reappeared, she got new shoes, and it was time for her to return to school. Each morning I trotted beside her on the dirt road, returning to the little brick farmhouse only after I had seen her safely to the edge of the schoolyard. There I waited, relaxing in the yard, guarding my household, during the day. Occasionally I chased a squirrel for amusement. I could see Bert and Ernie luxuriating on a windowsill, watching my playful antics with bored disdain. The cats rarely came outdoors. They were too concerned about muddying their paws or dampening their sleek fur with dew. Never in my life before or since have I met such a pair of vain and lazy creatures. Even so, I had an odd affection for the pair.

If the weather was unpleasant, I had simply to scratch politely at the kitchen door and Emily's mother would invite me inside. My bowl was always full of fresh water, and the kitchen smelled of herbs and newly baked bread.

What a happy, undemanding life! I remembered my lucrative days as a supermodel with no regret that they were ended, though I thought still of the photographer, when we were struggling to find our way in the world. I remembered dear Jack with affection and a touch of grief, but the days of shivering under flattened tin, of foraging for food in dumpsters, held no nostalgia for me. My earliest memories, of my sweet mother, remained a source of tender thoughts, and I forgave her for leaving us alone. I rarely thought of my quarrelsome, boisterous brothers at all.

It was only Wispy for whom I still yearned. Sometimes, watching Bert and Ernie, observing their admiration of and attachment to each other (egotistical though it was, since they were identical), I fell victim to an overwhelming sense of loss.

> *Once, long ago, I had a sister!*
> *Oh, can you imagine how I have . . .*

I couldn't quite get the second line right, since the only rhyme I could think of, *kissed her,* wasn't really accurate. But I enjoyed working on it, toying with the words in my mind as I lay drowsily in the sunny yard.

One morning it was raining. Dutifully I walked Emily to school. She was wearing a shiny slicker and boots and taking pleasure in wading through some of the puddles that had appeared in the uneven road. I tend to be somewhat fastidious about my appearance, and damp fur is extremely unattractive, so I did not take much pleasure in the morning walk. Once, back in the city, I had seen a Weimaraner dressed in a raincoat; it had seemed foolish at the time, but now, dripping as I was, I began to wonder whether perhaps a doggy slicker might not actually be a desirable thing.

Back at the house, I scratched at the door and was grateful, as Emily's mother dried me with a thick towel. She had been making cookies; I could smell the dough. I shook myself to rearrange and fluff my still-damp fur. On the kitchen counter, a small television was turned on. I am not a television fan, although I do enjoy reruns of the old *Lassie* shows. There is something about Lassie — the keen intelligence, the aristocratic bearing — that reminds me of my mother.

Actually, that's what I was thinking at that moment: how

much this scene was like an old *Lassie* rerun, with the dog entering the kitchen of the farmhouse, where Mom was baking cookies. Of course, there were no Siamese cats in the life of Lassie, and at this moment, Bert and Ernie were watching me through slitted eyes from their spot on the windowsill. There was also no television, I was thinking as I smoothed my own fur with my tongue, in Lassie's kitchen.

I circled my spot on the braided kitchen rug, lay down, and yawned.

Suddenly I heard, in whining unison from the cats, "It's Keeeeeeper!"

At the same moment I heard Emily's mother say in a startled voice, "Keeper!"

I raised my head, of course. Never before had the three of them at once called out my name.

To my surprise, they were not looking at me. They were staring at the television. Not wanting to leave my comfy spot on the rug, I craned my neck to get a better look at the small screen. A commercial was playing. I could see the rear end of a dog, its tail dangling in obvious discontent, walking away with a sort of contemptuous gait. Then the camera showed a woman tasting some low-fat yogurt, its brand clearly visible on the label, from a small carton. The woman licked her lips and smiled. "Well," she said to the camera, "*I* like it just fine!"

Emily's mother started to laugh. She closed the oven door after sliding the tray of cookies inside. She reached over and clicked the television off. The cats rearranged themselves, examined their paws, and closed their eyes again.

"That dog looked just like you, Keeper!" Emily's mother said. "Did you see him? He sneaked a taste of the yogurt, and then he made a face. Did you see how he sort of sneered and walked away?"

I hadn't seen anything except the rear end of the dog. It had looked, except for a bent section of the tail and a small patch of discolored fur on the hip, astonishingly like my own rear end, which I confess I have viewed occasionally in a mirror by twisting my body around carefully. From the description of the dog's facial expression, I could picture the sneer. It had been my famous sneer.

But I was quite certain the dog was not me. I had never made a yogurt commercial. The photographer had found a way to replace me with an imposter, a look-alike, a wannabe.

Or . . . ? Could it possibly be? My mind raced.

I searched my recollections from those earliest days, so long ago. I recreated visually the scenes from the alley: our cozy home behind the trash cans, our little litter cuddled there together. There I could see Wispy in my memory, the smallest among us, struggling always to find her place. She had looked so undernourished, so bedraggled, so appealing in her homeliness, with her fur unkempt and her tail not quite straight.

Suddenly I remembered with certainty and recognition the small patch of discolored fur on Wispy's left hip.

In disbelief I rushed over to the television set as if I could will the commercial to run again. But the screen was blank, the set dark and silent. Emily's mother had left the room. The only sounds in the farmhouse kitchen were the faint hum of the refrigerator, the snores of the two Siamese cats, and the rain falling against the windows.

I tried desperately to think what to do.

14

Oh, if only a dog could converse in human speech! Life would be so much easier. If we could write letters, send e-mail, pick up a telephone and communicate! Instead, when told, "Speak!" we put forth an abbreviated "Woof," which garners us a pat on the head and a biscuit.

I needed no praise or biscuits now. I needed information.

Pretending to be napping on the rug, I spent most of the day trying to figure out a way to find Wispy. I was quite certain it had been she in the commercial. No other dog in the world could be so much like me in mannerisms and yet at the same time have that familiar patch of discolored fur, that particular bend to the tail.

The only way was the one I did not want to undertake. I felt that by using my canine sense of direction, smell, and memory, I could very probably find my way back to the city where I had lived. It would take time, and I would have to make my way again through the woods, foraging, to reach the golf course from which I had fled. From there it would be even more difficult, but I know there have been cases where lesser dogs than I have followed car routes for many miles.

In the city, I could make my way to the photographer again. I knew that in his keeping I would find my sister, though how she had achieved the role as my replacement was beyond my powers of imagination.

But to make such a journey would mean leaving the little farmhouse and the family — even the cats — that I had come to love and call mine. What kind of Keeper would I be if I abandoned those dear ones who had taken me in?

There were moral questions involved.

I tossed and turned on the rug, groaning aloud as I wrestled with my options.

What is the answer? What is the way?
To leave? Remain? To go? To . . .

I was torn not only with indecision but with the frustrations of a poet looking for the right word. *Abide* didn't rhyme at all, though it had the right meaning. Being a poet is so difficult.

Bert and Ernie, watching me from the windowsill, finally expressed their impatience with my moral and literary struggles, even though they didn't know the cause of my agony.

"Geeeez," they whined in unison. "How can we sleeeep, with you making so much noise?" Finally they rose, looked at me in disgust, and went back upstairs to their alternative napping place.

When Emily came home from school, she knelt beside the place where I still lay on the rug. "You didn't meet me on the road," she said in concern. "What's the matter, Keeper?"

I lifted my head and looked into her solemn, trusting eyes. Poor child! She had no idea that I was wrestling with the idea of leaving her. The realization made me groan anew.

"Mom!" Emily called. "Something's wrong with Keeper! He's groaning! I think he's sick!" Her voice was worried, and she stroked my head gently.

Her mother hurried into the kitchen and knelt beside Emily. It was a lovely moment, lying there surrounded by humans who cared for me. My eyes actually filled with tears at the sweetness of it.

"Maybe he just has a cold," Emily's mother said. "His eyes are running. And he did sneeze this morning when he came in from the rain."

"But I think his stomach hurts, too," Emily said. "He was groaning a minute ago."

A plan began to form suddenly in my mind. Yes! I began to perceive a way in which I could find a route to my sister, and I would not have to survive in the woods, eating rabbit! It was suddenly quite clear to me what I must do.

I whimpered a little and rested my head uncomfortably on the bare floor.

Emily's mother rose and went to the refrigerator. "Let's see if he'll eat something," she suggested to Emily. "What does he like best? What would tempt him?"

"Not dogfood," Emily said. "He hates dogfood. Do we have any leftover macaroni and cheese? He loves macaroni and cheese."

Her mother looked at her suspiciously. "How do you know that?"

Emily blushed. "I fed him some, under the table," she confessed. "He really loved it."

Her mother sighed. But I could see, even from my reclining position with my half-closed, moist eyes, that she was removing the covered baking dish from the refrigerator.

"Should I put some in the microwave, do you think?" she asked Emily.

I groaned in reply. A dog doesn't need his food warmed. Cold macaroni and cheese was the finest treat I could imagine. I lifted my head and upped my ears slightly. I allowed my tail to thump pathetically against the floor.

"I don't think he cares," Emily said. "Just give it to him cold. See? He's looking better already."

I watched alertly while her mother scooped a lavish helping of macaroni and cheese into the bowl marked FIDO.

But as she set the bowl beside me, I remembered the plan that had come to me just a moment before. I remembered my sister. I knew that everything depended on my ability to withstand temptation at this moment.

It was excruciating. But with the bowl of macaroni within six inches of my mouth, with the smell of macaroni, and especially the smell of cheddar cheese, and a hint of Parmesan, permeating my nostrils, with wild desire palpitating in my very soul, I forced myself to turn away. It was perhaps my finest moment of renunciation. I groaned loudly, writhed a little, and placed my head miserably on the floor.

"That does it," said Emily's mother, and I could hear her lift the bowl and place it on the table. "He *is* sick. Put your raincoat back on, Emily. We're taking him to the vet."

She carried me to the car. I lay limp in her arms, as good an actor, I thought, as Lassie or Rin-Tin-Tin. I did feel a little guilty, deceiving them, but it was part of the plan that I hoped would serve us all well in the end.

15

EMILY'S MOTHER, LOOKING CONCERNED, lifted me gently
to the familiar stainless steel table and laid my unresponsive
body on the cold metal. Emily stood nearby, her nose level
with the tabletop, watching me, her face worried. I remained
limp, feigning serious illness. Feebly, I opened my eyes in order to ascertain that the veterinarian leaning over me was the
same one who had treated me so long ago in my previous life
as Pal. Sure enough, he was the same overweight, jolly man
with rimless glasses that I remembered from the earlier days.

So it was time to act. I jostled the doctor's arm and the
stethoscope aside and scrambled to an upright position.
Quickly, before he could restrain me, I assumed the posture

110

that I had affected in so many magazine photographs and television commercials: the studied, casual pose, head tilted, looking bored and above it all. Then slowly I lifted my upper lip. Majestically, I sneered.

Emily squealed in surprise. "It's the dog on the TV!"

Her mother, staring at me, said, "Keeper?"

But I did not resume my Keeper persona, not yet. I continued to sneer.

The veterinarian looked at me closely. He put his stethoscope down. "Where did you get this dog?" he asked Emily and her mother.

"Why, ah, he just —"

Emily interrupted. "He followed me home from school! And he didn't have a collar, so we couldn't . . ."

I dropped my sneer and listened intently. My ears were erect, and I'm certain that my eyes had an intelligent, querying look.

Thoughtfully, the doctor rubbed my fur. "He's not sick," he said, stating the obvious. "But he looks very familiar."

"Well, no wonder he looks familiar," Emily's mother said impatiently. "We brought him in here for his shots just last spring."

"No, no, of course I remember that. But he looks familiar in another way."

I sighed. Still on the table, I stood, repeating to myself what had become a sort of mantra of self-display.

Upright, my tail! Forward, my paws!

I tried to shed any remnant of the placid household pet and to show them that I had had a previous existence as a star. Of course I couldn't strut forward, or I would have fallen off the table onto the tile floor, defeating my purpose and destroying my own dignity. And the steel table made it difficult to stand properly, because there was no traction for my claws. But I posed the way I often had in my days as a supermodel: eyes forward, expression one of profound aloofness and disdain.

"*Pal?*" the veterinarian said suddenly. I turned my head in his direction and felt that we were on our way to revelation.

"*Keeper?*" Emily said in a puzzled voice. I turned my head to her, too. She raised her hand toward me and I licked it gently. It tasted of sweat and pocket fuzz, not a great combination. But it tasted of Emilyness, too.

The veterinarian went to his filing cabinet, the same cabinet from which he had, just a few minutes before, removed the medical records of a dog named Keeper. This time he rummaged until he found those of Pal. Carefully he compared the weight and description, glancing over at me from time to time as he studied the chart.

"He can't be that dog on the TV," Emily's mother said, "because just this morning I saw that dog in an ad for yogurt!"

"They run those ads over and over, Mom," Emily pointed out. Her voice was very glum. "Probably he made the yogurt ad months ago."

She could, of course, have been correct. But she wasn't. I had never made a yogurt commercial in my life. One does have one's standards.

"Will we have to give him back?" Emily asked in a small voice, and I could see that there were tears in her eyes.

The veterinarian, with Pal's chart and its information in his hand, went to the telephone and began to dial.

We drove home, back to the little ivy-covered farmhouse, and fed the cats, both of them wild with curiosity though they pretended to be blasé. Instead of the usual conversation at dinner between Emily and her mother, there was only the sound of forks against the plates. Occasionally someone said something about the weather, the way humans do when they are overwhelmed by situations. I sat before my bowl, that silly thing with FIDO painted on its side, and nibbled halfheartedly at my food. Gloom filled the kitchen.

In the morning all of us were silent in the car as we proceeded to the city. Each of us, I'm certain, was remembering with dismay the photographer's response to the veterinarian's phone call. He had been overjoyed to hear that I had been found. Yes, he had explained, he had found a substitute dog — a female, he said, confirming what I had known, that it was Wispy — but just think! Now he would have a pair of them! Picture the excitement in the world of advertising!

Emily sat in the back seat with me, and I placed my head in her lap so that she could stroke behind my ears. Gazing up at her, I saw that she was crying, preparing herself sadly to relinquish her beloved pet.

It was not what I had wanted, not at all what my intention had been. I had no desire to return to the photographer and my glamorous city life; those things were what I had run away from months before.

All I had wanted was to see my sister! But I had no way of telling anyone.

As we approached the familiar neighborhood, I lifted myself up and pressed my face against the window of the car. I confess that I gave an extra little lick to the glass, trying to leave as much of myself as possible behind with my family, even in the form of smeared spit. I was gratified to notice that there was dog hair on the seat as well, and a half-chewed rawhide bone lying forgotten on the floor.

I watched Toujours Cuisine slide by as we turned a corner,

and I whimpered, recognizing my birthplace there behind it, in the alley. How long ago it all seemed.

Not far away, Emily's mother, checking the written directions she'd been given, parked the car in front of the photographer's apartment building. He still lived in the same luxurious building; I could see that my family was impressed. Sighing, Emily clipped a newly purchased leash to my newly purchased collar. Thankfully, both were tasteful black leather, nothing with rhinestones or a monogram; still, they were a leash and a collar, and I had lived for so long now a free, unfettered country life. It made me sad. It made me inspired to compose.

Leash and collar, collar and leash
Make a dog look nouveau riche.

Oh, the irony of it! That under these most unfortunate and worrying circumstances I had put together, with no effort at all, what might have been one of my better poems! The reversed repetition in the first line, the incorporation of the second language, and the clever, clever rhyme —

But I had no time to ponder it further. My brave, beloved Emily held the end of the leash as we ascended in the elevator to the familiar eighth floor, and it was she who patted my head reassuringly as we waited for the photographer to respond to our knock on the door of 8-E.

But it was dear Wispy who, standing at the photographer's side, first looked at me, startled, then sniffed, and finally leaped in joyful recognition and yelped in delight at my return.

"What's going on?" the photographer asked as he and Emily and Emily's mother watched my sister and me roll ecstatically together on the floor. "I thought she'd be territorial and aggressive. I thought he'd be upset at seeing another dog here in his place."

"I thought he'd be frightened," Emily's mother said. "He seemed very nervous in the car."

"He wasn't nervous," Emily corrected. "He was depressed."

Wispy and I lay panting, side by side, our tails thumping rhythmically on the rug. I glanced over and saw that her tail, though it had improved substantially since her early days when it was so inadequate, was still considerably less magnificent than mine. I was a little relieved by that. A little guilty about my feeling of relief, I licked Wispy's face in apology.

She licked me back, and with Emily beside us, we lay happily together on the rug, talking of the past, while the adult humans shared some coffee and discussed the future.

16

"I was peeking out," I confessed to my sister, "when they took you away. I was under a piece of cardboard. And then I wanted to go, too, but by the time I ran after you, the door to the restaurant had closed and you were gone."

"You were brave to run after me," Wispy said.

"No," I confessed miserably, "I wasn't brave at all. I was a coward! I was hiding because I was frightened. But then I heard them say that you would go to a shelter and be put to sleep. I thought you'd have a nice raggedy blanket and a place next to a warm stove."

Wispy shook her head. "No," she said. "I had to stay in a cage. I got fleas. And the food was terrible."

"My food wasn't very good either," I said sympathetically. I told her about my time with Jack, how we foraged for food in dumpsters and trash cans. I told her about the rats, and saw her recoil in horror.

"I had fleas, too," I admitted, embarrassed.

The photographer had taken Emily's mother into the kitchen for coffee. In the background I could hear them talking. Emily lay on the floor with Wispy and me, her arms around us both. It was as if she could understand our conversation, though surely it must have been no more than grunts and whimpers to her human hearing.

"I didn't mind it there at the shelter," Wispy went on, "but it always made me sad when people came and took the other dogs away. Our brothers both got homes and families. The cook from the restaurant took Tug, and his friend was going to take Tussle, but he changed his mind. So they dropped both of us off at the shelter, and just a few days later someone came and picked Tussle as a birthday gift for his little boy. So Tussle got a family, too. But no one ever chose me." Her lip quivered a little.

She described how the spaniels, terriers, and shepherds in surrounding cages were admired and adopted, one by one. Shy as she was, it took Wispy a long time to make friends; and then, at the shelter, just as soon as she felt comfortable with a new companion, that one too would be chosen and taken away.

"Even cats," Wispy said in amazement. "Imagine that! People came and chose cats! They *chose* cats!"

What a humiliation it must have been for my sister. I groaned in sympathy.

"My time was almost up," she described. "You know, they

only keep you at the shelter for a limited period. Then you have to be destroyed."

I yelped. *"Destroyed?"*

Wispy nodded sadly. "It happens," she said.

I was shocked. I had not known. We stopped talking briefly, our heads bowed, and we shared a moment of silence in honor of all unwanted dogs. Well, cats, too.

"What saved you?" I asked.

"The man who ran the shelter. I think he was fond of me. I never complained about the food — I always ate nicely. I didn't bark much. And I tried to keep my cage as neat as possible. So after a while, he decided to let me stay. I think, actually, he was breaking the rules.

"And then one day the photographer came to the shelter. He was frantic. He said that he'd lost his very valuable dog . . ."

I sighed, savoring the word *valuable*. Wispy paused.

"Go on," I told her. "How did he describe me?"

"Well, I heard him say that you were a full-grown male, highly intelligent —"

"Did he actually say *highly?*"

"Yes, I'm certain he did. Highly intelligent, and well trained —"

"Did he mention my appearance in particular?"

"Yes, because he was asking the man who ran the shelter if perhaps someone had turned you in there. He said he was looking for a medium-sized, long-haired —"

"Just long-haired? He didn't say anything about the quality of the hair itself? He might have used the word *luxuriant*, perhaps?"

"Well, he might have, I suppose," said Wispy. "I don't remember all the details, exactly."

"Did he specify anything about the tail, by chance?" I asked, swishing my magnificent one from side to side as it lay on the rug.

Wispy swished hers in response. "Yes," she said. "I remember that particularly, because when the man in charge showed him around, he looked into all the cages, and he was so excited when he saw me! He cried out, 'My goodness! It's not the same dog, but they're so similar! Look at that tail!'"

I glanced back at hers as she was talking. Certainly it had improved greatly from the inadequacy of her puppy days. But it was still rather sparse, and it *did* have that bent end.

"Do you mean to say," I asked Wispy, trying to phrase the question tactfully, "that he compared your tail to mine?"

"Yes," she said cheerfully. "He was amazed at the similarity."

Oh, dear. I could feel that we might be on the verge of a very immature quarrel. I didn't want that to happen.

"Your tail," I said, "is, ah, certainly a very pleasing one. But in all honesty, I do feel that mine is more, shall we say, well endowed."

"Mine has character, though, don't you think?" she asked, very sweetly.

Well, I could certainly concede that. "Yes," I told her. "Yours has definite character."

Quarrel averted, she continued. The story was quite simple. The photographer had taken Wispy home. He had trained and groomed her to be my successor.

To my surprise, Wispy said she enjoyed the work as a model. She didn't mind the long hours, the constant combing, the bright lights that tended to dry one's fur (of course, hers had never been terribly luxuriant anyway). Their life together, hers and the photographer's, had been successful and congenial. It would have continued unchanged had I not appeared at their front door.

"Here's what Christopher and I have decided!" The voice interrupted our pleasant little conversation on the rug. Wispy and I looked up at Emily's mother. Emily did, too.

Christopher? I thought. Then I realized that must be the photographer's name.

"We'll take Keeper back home with us," she said, and Emily's face lit up. I suppose mine did, too. It was what I really wanted, to be back in the farmhouse with my family, now that I knew Wispy was safe and well cared for.

"That's my name — Keeper," I whispered to my sister.

"Mine's Sal," she whispered back, giggling with embarrassment.

"But when Christopher needs him for a special assignment with two dogs, he can borrow him," Emily's mother went on.

The photographer had come to stand beside her and was listening. "And on weekends," he added, "when Sal and I aren't working, we'll come out to the country to get some fresh air and so that the dogs can play together, since they appear to be such good friends."

Wispy (I will never bring myself to call her Sal) looked at me in delight. She nuzzled my neck affectionately, and I licked her ear.

17

I**T DOES SOUND LIKE A SATISFYING ENDING**, doesn't it? The long-lost brother and sister are reunited. The little girl keeps her much-loved pet. The deserving mother meets an attractive and well-to-do man. Plans are made for the future. People smile. Tails wag.

But those with a literary bent and a keen eye for plot (and I must count myself among them, expanding now as I am from the world of poetry into the broader, more demanding realm of narrative) will have perceived an unresolved thread.

As we prepared to leave the photographer's apartment, Wispy (I will never call her Sal) whined, and the photographer reached for her leash, which was hanging from a hook in the kitchen.

"She needs to go out," he said. "I'll walk you down to your car."

"Keeper?" Emily asked, looking at me, "do you want to go out, too?"

Going out, I should explain, is a euphemism for taking care of bodily functions.

I wagged my tail and looked eager.

"Well," Emily's mother suggested, "why don't we walk the dogs before we start back? It's a long drive."

So for the first time in many months, I found myself walking the streets of my old neighborhood at the end of a leash. The difference was that now it was my beloved Emily at the other end instead of a minimally talented, unemployed actor from Madison, Wisconsin.

I yearned again for the power of speech. I wanted to tell Emily of my beginnings; I wanted to show her my birthplace, to confide in her that Wispy (I will never call her Sal) was not just a look-alike mongrel with a bent tail but in fact my full-blooded sister, companion of my heart.

How I wished, turning a familiar corner, that I could point out sadly the spot where I had so often sat with Jack, cajoling passersby to drop coins into his cupped hands so that we could survive another day.

"Is this a good restaurant?" I heard Emily's mother ask the photographer casually, pausing as we passed the carved door of Toujours Cuisine. He nodded.

"Not bad," he told her. "When you have more time someday, we can go there for dinner."

"When we don't have the dogs along." She laughed.

Ah, if only she knew! Wispy (I will never call her Sal) glanced at me and we smiled. The memories of French food!

"*Selle d'agneau roti*," I murmured to my sister.

"*Ragouts de veau*," she replied knowingly.

What a pleasant afternoon it was, combining as it did the smells and sounds of the city, the contentment of good human company, the rapture of my sister by my side, and the happy memories of earlier days.

Then something evil intruded. Nose, ears, eyes came into play in the correct order. I smelled Scar first: the acrid, unwashed scent of enemy. Then my ears perceived his low, menacing growl. I stood still, on full alert.

Finally I spotted him. Across the street, next to a newspaper rack, I saw his flattened, hostile face, his grime-streaked neckless body, the thick legs and ugly tail stump. He had not changed. And I could tell, from the look and smell of him, and from his throaty growl, that he recognized me. His desire to destroy me had obviously been rekindled.

Emily's mother and the photographer were still reading the menu displayed in front of the restaurant. Emily, my leash loose in her relaxed hand, had leaned down and was patting Wispy (never Sal), talking to her in a quiet, loving voice. No one but I had noticed the threat.

My original promise, my pledge to defeat Scar someday, surfaced in my memory. I had, over the intervening months, written better verse because I had matured as a poet. But this one, recalled now, still seemed my most valiant, most heroic effort. I repeated it to myself now.

> *I vow this, Scar, with all my might!*
> *Someday I'll beat you in a fight!*

We were separated by the width of the street, and he was watching me malevolently. I was no longer a cringing, intimidated puppy pleading for breakfast. I was no longer an adolescent itching for a nighttime brawl. Now I was a splendid full-grown dog with teeth (I exposed them to him) like carved granite, an unwavering growl (I gave him only a low hint of its magnitude), and a massive, fully muscled body ornamented at its end with a tail of unequaled grandeur.

Demanding homage, and willing to battle for it, I pulled my leash loose from Emily's grasp and inched forward, waiting for the right moment. Then the unthinkable happened. Oblivious to traffic or to onlookers, the hideous dog gathered himself and charged, exploding from his stance and thundering across the street with his teeth bared.

But he was charging for Emily.

With no other thought than to save my beloved human child, I leapt toward Scar and intercepted him, grab-

bing his throat with my teeth tight around his repulsive flesh. He snarled in hatred and we locked in mortal combat, aware that only one of us would emerge alive. From what seemed a far distance, I heard Emily and her mother both scream.

Then I heard the roaring sound of a truck approaching at full speed; there was the sudden screech of brakes, a thud, and I felt Scar torn from my grip and saw him disappear under the massive wheels. I felt no pain, but had an awareness that I, too, was hit and caught by the huge undercarriage of the vehicle. The noise was terrible: ripping, rattling sounds, human shouts, and a piercing shriek that may even have been my own. I no longer knew. By then everything was chaotic and confused; a second later, it simply turned to black silence and oblivion.

I surfaced to consciousness and pain several times in the next few days, then drifted again into merciful sleep. When, finally, I was more alert and able to keep my eyes open, I could see that I was once again in the familiar office of the veterinarian. They had me housed in a comfortable pen, with a bowl of water near my head and a clean blanket folded beneath my bruised, aching body.

The veterinarian, the very one who had identified me less than a week before, entered the pen when he saw that I was awake. He felt my pulse, looked at my eyes carefully, and talked to me in a comforting voice.

"Is it Pal?" he asked, and when I sighed, he tried again. "Keeper?"

At the sound of my true name, Keeper, I blinked and tried to lift my head. The doctor stroked my fur gently. "You got pretty badly banged up," he told me. The information was unnecessary. I could feel it. It was excruciatingly painful just to move.

"But you're going to be okay," he said, still stroking my neck. "You're going to heal. And," he added, "you're a hero. You saved the little girl. You saved Emily."

At the sound of that precious name, I lifted my head high, despite the pain. The doctor smiled. "She's in the other room, waiting to see you," he said. "They all are. Your whole family, even that female who looks so much like you. What's her name? Sal?"

I whimpered a bit and rested my head on the blanket again. I would never call her Sal. But I guessed all humans would, and I would have to accept that.

I hoped my family hadn't brought Bert and Ernie with them. I needed commiseration, but not the kind of saccharine *faux* sympathy I knew the cats would delight in providing.

"Okay, Keeper," the doctor went on, "I'm going to let them come in for a little visit. You take it easy, though. Don't try to stand up. You're going to have a tough time balancing for a while. But you'll adjust. It won't take long. Before you know it, you'll be home again and as good as new."

Then he hesitated. "Well, maybe not as good as new, Keeper. You'll be *different*. But you're still a healthy, heroic dog. I want you to remember that."

Then, as he paused before getting to his feet, he explained the specific nature of my terrible injury. The shock was almost overwhelming. My thoughts were confused, and I began to take deep breaths, trying to control myself and get my bearings again.

A poem, I thought. *I must write a poem now, to help me through this.*

But it was impossible. Even poetry was gone from me now.

I lay there suffering, not from my wounds but from the terrible new knowledge of my loss, and heard him tell my family to come in.

I had been brave in the presence of the doctor, I think; and in the embrace of my human family, who had not brought the cats, I continued to maintain an admirably proud and stoic pose. I accepted their pats and kisses and their sympathy with dignity and affection.

But finally, in the privacy of my visit with my sister (for my human family had nudged her into my pen and then tactfully retreated, leaving us alone together), I broke down. At first, holding my head erect to look at the loving, sympathetic gaze of my homely but faithful sibling, I tried to maintain a devil-may-care attitude.

"Forward my feet!" I declaimed. *"Upright my —"*

But I lost control then, and howled with grief.

"Wispy," I wailed, "I have lost my glorious tail!"

She nuzzled my neck and licked my chin for comfort.

"You still have a glorious tale," she reminded me gently. "Why don't you tell it?"

And so I have.